SILK SHADOW

BLACKTHORN SECURITY
BOOK THREE

GEMMA FORD

CHAPTER 1

*V*iper arrived at Blackthorn Security headquarters in Washington D.C. at precisely 0900 hours. His shirt was crisp and immaculate, his suit, while not from Madison Avenue, was the finest he could afford. His shoes gleamed so brightly that he could see his reflection in them. He wanted to look the part. This was the most important meeting of his career, and he couldn't afford to screw it up.

"Don't worry, Pat's a good guy," Blade had told him during his surprise visit last week. "I served with his son over in Afghanistan."

Viper wasn't so sure. He'd heard that Pat was a hard man to get to know. Stubborn and unflinching when it came to picking and choosing their operations, absolutely incorruptible, and a force to be reckoned with. Rumor had it that he even made the smooth-talking politicians on Capitol Hill quake in their boots. A man to be admired, but it did make him rather formidable. But then, he'd expect nothing less from a former SEAL Commander.

Pat's reputation preceded him. He'd built Blackthorn Security into an organization steeped in secrecy and rumor.

His operatives were all ex-military, mostly spec ops, and they got the job done. Their success rate was through the roof, which was a lot more than could be said for most private security companies.

Viper had researched them thoroughly after Blade's visit.

Blade Wilson.

Now there was a blast from the past. He'd never thought he'd see that mountain of a man again, not since the SEAL's last op in Afghanistan where his entire team bar one had been taken out. After that, Blade had bailed on the military—medical discharge—and the last Viper had heard, he'd gone missing—presumed dead—in the Middle East during an off-the-books assignment.

"I thought you were dead," he'd told him through a God-almighty hangover, when his old acquaintance had appeared at his door a couple of days ago.

Blade had snorted. "Takes more than a few angry Taliban soldiers to put me down. I heard you were out and thought I'd pop over for a cup of joe. You going to invite me in?"

Viper didn't have much choice. Blade was blocking his doorway and didn't look like he was going to move any time soon.

"Sure, why not? I could use one myself."

"Rough night?"

Viper ran a hand through his disheveled hair and winced at the tender spot on the side of his head. He'd literally peeled himself off the couch five minutes ago.

"Nasty graze you got there. How'd it happen?"

"I think someone hit me over the head with a bottle," he complained, feeling it with his finger. "But it's a bit hazy."

Blade studied him. "Bar fight?"

A shrug. "Something like that."

They walked into the kitchen where Viper poured two

cups of coffee from a freshly made pot. He didn't even ask if he wanted cream, just handed it to him black.

No cream in the Middle East. They'd all gotten used to drinking it black.

Viper turned to face his buddy, still confused as to why he was here. "So, you were just passing through the neighborhood and thought you'd look me up?"

"Yeah, and I've got a proposition for you."

Viper sat down a little unsteadily. His head was pounding, but he couldn't decide if it was because of his hangover or the dent in his hairline. "A proposition? What kind of proposition?"

Blade sat opposite him at the kitchen table. "I heard you'd been making a bit of a nuisance of yourself." He'd always been very direct. Not one to beat around the bush.

"Who told you that? I was helping a damsel in distress. Some guy was laying into her. I just shoved him off." And got a bottle in the head as a screw you.

Blade glanced at the wound that Viper hadn't even bothered to clean up yet. It was still seeping, despite the scab beginning to form. "Something tells me he didn't appreciate it."

Viper winced. "You could say that. The cops didn't appreciate my good will either. Spent half the night in lockup."

Blade sipped his coffee contemplatively.

"What's going on, Viper?" he asked after a pause. "This isn't like you. You're a SEAL sniper for God's sake, you take out the enemy from a distance. You don't go around looking for bar fights."

"I told you, I was helping—"

"Yeah, I know what you said. It's just unlike you, that's all. Are you bored or something?"

Viper stared into his coffee, still gently swirling from where he'd stirred it. A long moment passed where he said nothing at all. When he finally spoke, his voice was a hoarse whisper. "I'm so freakin' bored, I'm thinking about putting a bullet through my head."

"Jesus, man. Why don't you get help?"

"Hey, don't panic. I'm not suicidal, not really. I just don't know what to do with myself. I thought about getting a job, but I'm not qualified for anything, except maybe working on the oil rigs up in Alaska. I don't want to be a fucking security guard at a shopping mall. This not knowing what to do is killing me." He ground his jaw and clutched his mug so hard he thought it might break.

"That's why I'm here," Blade said.

Viper glanced up.

"I've got a job for you."

He frowned. "Where?"

"Where I work, at Blackthorn Security."

"You work for *them*?" Everyone on the private security circuit knew about Blackthorn Security. Ex-Special Ops guys on off-the-book assignments for the U.S. government, as well as some private clients. Most of the time, they were talked about in hushed tones with a degree of reverence usually reserved for legends in the field.

"Yeah, I'm the Ops Manager. I started the company with Pat Burke after I got back from Afghanistan. I was in a dark place, and he came to me with his idea, and we took it from there."

Viper stared at him. "I had no friggin' idea, man."

"Not many people do."

"So, what does the esteemed Blackthorn Security want with me?"

"We have a job that requires your particular skill set, and we're pretty swamped at the moment. Business is booming and we're still recruiting operatives. There's a lot of bad crap going down in the world."

Viper scoffed. Blade didn't have to tell him that. He'd been involved in more than his fair share of it over the last decade.

"You've done personal protection work before, haven't you? I seem to remember you guarding those oil engineers out in Iraq a couple of years back."

"Yeah, although that was a sideline. A special favor for the Navy." He shrugged. "You know my skillset is somewhat different."

"I know." Blade gave a slow grin. "That's what makes you perfect for this job. We've got a client who needs close protection around the clock. She's a very important client, a personal friend of Pat's, and she's been getting death threats."

"Who is it?"

"Doesn't matter. It's a job. We could really use your help on this one, man. If all goes well, we'll sign you on full-time. Pension plan, dental, the works. We have ops all over the world. It's a great opportunity."

Viper hadn't had to think about it for long.

After Blade had left, he'd showered, gone to the nearest walk-in clinic and got three stitches in his head, then called Blade back and accepted.

CHAPTER 2

His stitches had been removed yesterday, and while his scar was still red and ugly, it was healing fast and was partially covered by his hairline.

"Wait here," the receptionist told him and picked up the phone. "Your nine o'clock's arrived, sir."

She smiled at Viper and stood up. "Follow me, Mr. Morgan."

They walked through a set of thick, glass security doors and down a short corridor. His shiny shoes sank into the plush carpeting as he gazed out of large, spotless windows on the right-hand side that overlooked a busy street. In the distance, the imposing structure of Fort Bragg loomed, a reminder of their roots and the disciplined precision that underpinned their operations.

The receptionist knocked on a door, then opened it without waiting for a reply. Shooting him a professional smile, she said, "Mr. Burke will see you now."

Viper took a deep breath. It stilled his nerves, not that he really had any. Calm, control, stillness—the traits of a sharp-shooter. He'd learned years ago how to silence his mind, vanquish his nerves, wait patiently for the shot. He used the same technique now, as he nodded his thanks, then when he was ready, went inside.

The Commander stood up. At over six foot with a face made of granite, he looked every bit the tough former SEAL Commander he was reputed to be. "Ah, Victor Morgan—or do you prefer Viper?"

"Viper, sir."

A nod. They shook hands. "I've heard good things about you. Excellent job in rescuing those hostages in Colombia. Could have been much worse than it was, if not for your brave act."

Viper shrugged it off. "I did what anyone in my position would have done, sir."

Pat locked his dark eyes on him. "Nonetheless, it was very well done. I'm sorry you got discharged over it. How are you feeling?"

"Fine. Never been in better shape."

"Bullet wounds all healed up?"

He nodded. "Weeks ago."

Pat's gaze lifted to the wound on his temple.

Viper held his tongue. The Blackthorn Security boss would have been told about his little bar fight and stint in the holding cell down at the Cumberland County Sheriff's Office. Too bad, there was nothing he could do about that now. Would it scupper his chances? He sure as hell hoped not.

He needed this job. It was more than just a job—it was a lifeline. Blackthorn Security. Hell, he would be lucky enough to be offered a position as a PPO at any firm, let alone here.

"Is that going to be a problem for you?" Pat asked pointedly.

"No, sir. It won't happen again."

Pat nodded and moved on. Viper exhaled.

"I think Blade explained what we need?"

He nodded. "Yes, sir. You need a personal protection officer for a client."

"A personal friend," he corrected. "I knew her mother."

"Yes, sir."

"And I understand you're keen to take on the role?"

"Yes, sir."

Please...

He clenched his fists under the table.

Pat nodded and looked him up and down. "Your reputation speaks for itself. If you're in agreement, then we can sign you on for a trial run. One op, and then we'll take it from there. How does that sound?"

Viper hissed out a slow breath. "That sounds good."

Pat slid a document over the desk toward Viper. "It says this is a probationary phase, and after this assignment ends, we'll make you a permanent offer. Short and sweet. I didn't have time to go into detail. You know the risks, you've done this before."

He gave a stoic nod, picked up a pen, and signed on the dotted line.

"Excellent." Pat grinned, and the granite cracked a little. He seemed less intimidating now. "I believe our client is waiting, so you can meet her right away."

"She's here, now?" Viper sat up straighter.

"Yeah, I asked her to come in so I could introduce you."

He'd been so sure Viper would say yes. That stung a little, but then, who wouldn't? It was Blackthorn Security. He'd be a fool not to accept the position.

Pat picked up the phone. "Show her in, Maisie."

A few minutes later, the office door swung open, and—Holy hell!—in walked the most stunning woman Viper had ever seen. Tall, close to five foot ten, with legs that stretched all the way to Canada, a Marilyn Monroe hour-glass figure, and features that could grace the cover of a magazine.

He was momentarily speechless. Then he stumbled to his feet.

Pat reached out an arm. "Izzy, come on in. I want you to meet your assigned personal protection officer, Viper Morgan."

The woman walked in and looked him over. Her expressive brown eyes studied his face lingering on his mouth, then dropped to his chest, flickered briefly over his biceps, before lowering to his legs. Now knew how women felt when guys ogled them. Right now he felt like a piece of meat on display.

She gave a little nod, as if to say, "you'll do", then stuck out her hand. "Izzy Beaumont. Good to meet you." Her voice was like cut glass, posh and crystal clear.

He puffed out his chest,—May as well look the part—forced a smile and engulfed her proffered hand in his hard, rough one. Her skin was soft, her nails perfectly manicured. A sensual exotic fragrance wafted over him. Floral, with a hint of something alluring. Vanilla, maybe. His gaze met hers. "Likewise."

She dropped her eyes first, pulling her hand away. He waited until she'd sat down, then resumed his seat.

"I take it you've told him about the death threats?" Her question was directed at Pat, but she was annoyed, he could hear it in her voice. Because he hadn't let her get the upper hand, or because she didn't want a bodyguard to begin with?

"Briefly. Why don't you fill him in on the details?"

The stunner turned to Viper. He tried not to stare at her long, smooth legs ending in high-heeled sandals, or the coral nail polish on her toes. The short summer dress she wore had risen up around her thighs. He had a fleeting image of those legs wrapped around him.

What the fuck?

Where had that thought come from?

He hardly knew the woman. Swallowing, he banished the indecent image to the furthest recesses of his mind.

"I don't know if you're aware, Mr. Morgan, but my father, Richard Beaumont, recently passed away."

"I'm sorry," he said. He didn't have a clue who Richard Beaumont was.

"Thank you." She paused, studying him. "To give you some background, he was the founder and CEO of Omega Enterprises, a mining conglomerate with interests in Mexico and Central America. When he died, he left the company to me. I am now the majority shareholder."

Viper had heard of Omega Enterprises. Money and power. That was quite a responsibility for one so young. She looked maybe twenty-four, twenty-five, which made her eight or nine years younger than him.

"I think these death threats are related to that."

"Do you have them with you?" Viper asked.

"No, I gave them to the police."

"There are copies in Miss Beaumont's file," Pat informed him.

Viper nodded. He'd look them up later.

"Anyway, the police believe I've got to take them seriously, so I sought out Pat, who said he could help. I understand you have prior experience in this area?"

Viper nodded. "Yes, ma'am."

"Okay, good. Well, I'd like you to start immediately, if possible. I'm leaving for San Diego tomorrow. It's kind of a working vacation, and I want you to come."

Viper glanced at Pat, who nodded. "Don't worry, Viper is ready to accompany you. We'll have to sort out the license for his weapon, but otherwise, he's good to go."

Guess he was going to San Diego.

Izzy smiled, the first time since she'd walked into the

room. "It's a fashion shoot for my new swimwear line. To be honest, I could do with a break. It's been a very trying few weeks."

"I'm sure." Pat smiled fondly. "Have fun and don't worry about a thing. Viper is as good as they come. You're in safe hands." When he wasn't drinking himself into a coma and getting involved in bar fights, yes.

She arched a perfectly shaped brow. "You can pick me up at five o'clock tomorrow morning. We fly out at seven-thirty."

"I'll need a list of those traveling with you," Viper said. "In order to vet them."

She hesitated, then nodded. "Of course, I'll see my assistant gets that off to you ASAP."

Her assistant?

He was battling to reconcile the swimwear line with the mining conglomerate. What did one have to do with the other? But he kept his questions to himself. All would be revealed in time when he had a chance to look over her file.

"See you tomorrow, then, Miss Beaumont."

She gave a terse nod, then turned to his boss. "Thank you, Uncle Pat. I appreciate your help."

Uncle?

Damn. When Blade had said friend of the family, he wasn't kidding.

Pat came around the desk and embraced her. If he was embarrassed by her term of endearment, he didn't show it. "Any time, Izzy. You know that."

Viper's eyes widened even further. Human contact from the formidable Pat Burke. Who would have thought it?

Izzy Beaumont swept out in her cloud of designer perfume.

"She's quite something, isn't she?" mused Pat, staring after her. "Done remarkably well for herself since her mother's death."

"It must be challenging, running the mining conglomerate."

Pat laughed, deep and growly. "Izzy's got her own fashion empire. She's what they call an influencer, I believe. Not that I'm one for social media."

Viper's eyes widened.

"She's got millions of followers. That makes her a very important asset to fashion brands. She's got her own swimwear line, as you heard, and a signature perfume. I understand she's in talks for other ventures too. Quite the entrepreneur, is our Izzy."

Our Izzy?

"You're related to her, sir?"

Pat's eyes flickered. "Not in the traditional sense, but I've known Izzy since she was a baby, and as her parents are both dead, I feel a certain responsibility toward her. She's my goddaughter."

Goddaughter.

Holy crap. He'd better not screw up.

Viper cleared his throat. "Thank you, sir, for the opportunity. I'm honored to be working for Blackthorn Security."

Pat shook his hand. "Glad to have you on board." His hair was turning silver at the sides, but he was still a rock of a man. Stocky and broad, he was built like a wrestler and clearly worked out regularly in the gym. Even his handshake was crushing. "Maisie will show you to your desk, where you can prep for tomorrow. There's quite a bit more on Izzy and her father's company in the file, and you should check out her Instagram profile—see what all the hype is about." He masked a grin. "I think you'll be surprised."

CHAPTER 3

*V*iper was assigned a desk in Blackthorn Security's headquarters' open-plan office. It was a wide, spacious area, surrounded by glass windows through which he could see the outline of the Washington Monument in the distance. It was a far cry from Fort Bragg, where he'd been based while in the Navy.

Thinking about it always left a pang. Hell, he missed it, but after being medically discharged, he couldn't go back. Now, finally, he had a purpose again. Even if it did come in a five-foot ten bombshell of a package.

Based in the office were a handful of support staff. They laid the groundwork and provided intelligence and logistics for the operatives out in the field. Big screens showed satellite and drone images, flight and shipping data, and one woman sat with earphones on, gazing at a telephone transcript flickering across her computer.

It felt very much like the ops center back at the Naval Special Warfare base, just with air conditioning and better furniture. He logged onto the computer and pulled up Izzy's file. It made for interesting reading.

Apparently, her father was something of a legend in mining circles. He'd ventured into Mexico when nobody else thought it worth the risk. Regions with complex regulatory environments, but a wealth of untapped resources. Beaumont had grown up in Oaxaca, thanks to his parents being part of the U.S. diplomatic corps, stationed at the U.S. Consulate in Oaxaca, and consequently, had a feel for how things worked there. His methods weren't always orthodox, and there were rumors of bribery and palm-greasing, particularly in the more corrupt areas.

Viper arched an eyebrow. That was often the way in that part of the world. Despite this, Beaumont had navigated the challenges and significantly expanded opportunities for modern mining companies to set up operations.

Generally, his projects were welcomed due to the massive investment of capital in the region. Not only that, but he also developed infrastructure, including roads and port facilities, making it easier to transport materials from the mines to export points. He created jobs and launched initiatives to help the local communities, such as building clinics, schools, and ensuring a reliable water supply.

A maverick, but a good guy.

It seemed his daughter had inherited his solid work ethic.

Beaumont had died in a car wreck driving from the mountains of the Sierra Madre, where the mine was located, to the coastal city of Mazatlán. According to the police report, he'd lost control of the vehicle and driven off a cliff into a steep ravine. No chance of survival. The inquiry ruled it an unfortunate accident.

He'd never operated in Mexico itself, but he'd been on a few ops in Central and South America, and none of them had gone according to plan. In the SEALs, they had a running joke: don't get too attached to Plan A, because it was usually Plan B or Plan C that you ended up executing. Plan A was a best-case scenario, and in that part of the world, he wasn't sure such a thing even existed.

Richard Beaumont's death was a tragic loss, by all accounts.

Now Izzy was at the helm. From what he could gather, she wasn't all that interested in her father's company. She had her own empire to manage. Her face had lit up when she'd talked about the swimsuit shoot. It was clear she cared about what she did. There was no smile when she'd spoken about the mining conglomerate.

Viper read the death threats—scanned copies of the original letter-sized notes. Sent to the victim by mail, they contained several short, threatening sentences.

Montezuma is not your problem.

Back off now, before you get hurt.

You don't belong here.

The messages got more threatening and more desperate as they progressed. There were six in total, the last one being the most ominous.

You've been warned.

Montezuma. That was the name of the mine in the mountains of Mexico.

He took a deep breath.

Izzy had done well not to panic. She'd kept her cool, even with this hanging over her head. He was impressed by her toughness.

Next, he checked her Instagram profile. He didn't have an Instagram account, but he had buddies who did. Two of them were in the fitness industry, running military-style boot camps for civilians so it made sense to market online. Another manufactured military apparel, waterproof kit, and wet weather gear. Whenever he wanted to feel sorry for himself, he logged on and browsed their profiles.

Proof you could have a successful life outside of the military.

Proof he'd failed.

"Whoa!"

He blinked as a startling array of colorful photographs appeared on the screen. Hell, it looked like a series of shots from a glossy travel magazine. Izzy laughing as she stood by a low, stone wall overlooking an idyllic Tuscan landscape. An infinity pool with Izzy in a swimsuit staring out toward the horizon. Izzy standing in a cobblestone alleyway in an unpronounceable European town in a flowing peach dress.

Always coifed. Always smiling. Always stunning.

He zoomed in on one of the photographs, a particularly fetching one of Izzy in a white bikini with black straps, her body glistening in the sun, the ocean shimmering behind her.

"Hello, I'm Anna. You must be Viper."

He flushed, wishing he could close the browser, but it would be too obvious now. He had to brazen it out. Pretend it was research, which it was. A woman with blonde hair in a ponytail was smiling down at him. Anna? That was Cole's wife. He'd done a few ops with Cole back in the day. Great guy. Reliable as they came. The private security world was small. Around here, almost everyone had met or worked with everyone else at some point or another.

"Hi, great to meet you, Anna. Blade told me you worked here. Logistics, isn't it?"

"Yes, that's right. Cole was thrilled when Blade told him you were joining the crew. We're so glad to have you on board. I know you'll fit right in." She was so nice, she put him at ease. Any apprehension he'd felt at working for the prestigious Blackthorn Security dissipated.

Her gaze flickered to his screen. "Izzy Beaumont is amazing. I follow her account. She's pretty inspirational."

He arched an eyebrow. "She is?"

"Yeah, she built her own brand from the ground up. She started out as a social media influencer—"

At his puzzled expression, she elaborated. "You know, someone who is famous for their lifestyle and fashion sense."

"Got it."

"But she always had a unique style. Her following grew, and soon teens around the world were trying to mimic her look. She does a great job of mixing haute couture with affordable mall fashion."

Whatever that meant.

"Then the top brands began to take notice, and soon she was a brand ambassador for a handful of designers and department stores. With the economy in the mess it's in, she was doing for them what retail no longer could. Then last year, she launched her swimwear line. Sexy, elegant swimsuits for real women." She gave a self-deprecating laugh. "I've got one—they're really flattering, actually. Anyway, the collection did so well, she's thinking about expanding into fashion. And she's got her own signature perfume. Silk, it's called. It smells incredible."

He wondered if that was what she'd been wearing in their meeting.

"She's certainly been busy." He turned back to the screen. Every photo had thousands of likes and almost as many comments. He could see why the brands loved her. "Two million, seven hundred forty-five thousand and fifty-three followers," he read.

"Insane, isn't it?" Anna shook her head. "But then the world needs style icons, especially ones who look like real women and not stick figures."

He studied Izzy's smiling face as she laughed into the camera, her head tilted back, long dark hair caressing the surface of the water. In this shot, she was standing waist-deep in the sea, her sun-kissed body gleaming, her glorious breasts rising above the bikini. The golden girl frolicking around in glamorous settings, living a life that other girls only dreamed about.

His principal. The woman he'd sworn to protect.

"Couldn't agree with you more," he muttered.

CHAPTER 4

*I*zzy was looking forward to this trip. They were shooting next season's swimwear collection, and the late August sunshine was just what she needed. It had been a tough few weeks arranging her father's funeral, taking over the reins at Omega Enterprises, and dealing with the threatening notes, while still running her own business.

Even tougher looking like you're having fun when you're expecting a sniper to take a shot at you at any moment. Okay, that was a bit ridiculous— it was probably just some prankster—but she couldn't be sure.

Uncle Pat had been a darling. Not really her uncle, but a close family friend. She'd called him that ever since she was a toddler, and old habits were hard to break. Besides, he felt like family.

She'd never quite gotten to the bottom of his relationship with her mother, although she knew they'd been close. If it wasn't for Pat's wife dying and seeing how distraught he'd been, she might have suspected they were more than friends.

And now she had Viper. What kind of name was that anyway?

She thought about the mysterious ex-military man with the hardened body of a soldier and eyes the color of the ocean. Pat had told her he'd done something quite brave in South America recently, although he hadn't gone into detail. Apparently, the former military man had been badly injured and as a result, medically discharged.

Safe hands, Pat had said.

She couldn't ignore those hands—scarred, calloused, and rough. Hands that had handled weapons and taken lives. How many lives, she wondered? Despite the late summer sun, Izzy felt a chill crawl up her spine.

She exited her apartment building, pulling her carry-on behind her. Lewis, the concierge, carried her two big suitcases downstairs. Inside were two weeks' worth of designer and department store brands she was contracted to show off while on vacation.

Her legions of followers liked that she wore clothes for real women. Not supermodels or anorexic celebrities, but women with curves and flaws and boobs. She showed them that they could also look sexy and elegant. Yesterday's imperfect was today's perfect.

Her bodyguard stood by the car, massive chest bursting out of a suit and tie, making it look almost ridiculous. Was it her imagination or did he appear even bigger and bulkier than yesterday? Then she noticed the protective vest beneath that pressed white shirt. He glanced up and down the street, alert and on guard. There was a Bluetooth listening device in his ear, presumably to call for help if needed.

The reality of her situation hit home. Her stomach clenched with a sudden spurt of anxiety.

Breathe.

She couldn't let this unknown threat ruin her life.

Viper was the best. He would protect her, until the police caught the person or organization behind those letters.

Please let it be soon.

Living like this wasn't going to be easy.

She descended the steps outside her apartment block and came to a stop beside him on the sidewalk. He towered over her, his hulking frame blocking out the early morning sun that had just poked its golden head over the D.C. skyline that counted as the horizon around here. Feeling awkward, she managed a tight smile.

"Morning, ma'am. Let me get that for you." He took the case from her, his hand brushing hers, but his gaze remained on his surroundings. A waft of manly aftershave floated her way, fresh and enticing, mingling with her own brand. The perfumer she'd worked with on Silk, her own fragrance, had taught her how to distinguish between different notes. Then there was that chiseled jaw, freshly shaven but somehow still hinting of a five o'clock shadow.

"Thank you."

Lewis placed the two heavy cases on the sidewalk beside the car. Viper lifted them up like they weighed no more than a child's school case. He was going to be useful in more ways than one.

"Ready, ma'am?" Viper asked.

She nodded. "Yes, but please call me Izzy, or if we're around people, Miss Beaumont. I'm not a politician or royalty."

"Yes, Miss Beaumont."

She climbed into the back. He got into the driver's seat, checked she was buckled in, then started the engine. Signaling, he pulled out into the traffic. Izzy settled back and concentrated on her phone. The drive to the airport would take half an hour—time to catch up on her emails.

They stopped at a traffic light. She looked up and accidentally met his gaze in the rearview mirror—an intense blue laser that cut through the air between them. Unnerved, she glanced away.

Something about him made her nervous, something she couldn't put her finger on. Sure, he was the strong silent type, but he seemed distant, like he carried a heavy burden behind those slanting sea-blue eyes. Behind the granite façade was a repressed strength that made her both fear and admire him. He was a killer—a sniper, Pat had said—but also her protector. A confusing contradiction.

Letting out a slow breath, she contemplated the trip ahead. Warm Californian sunshine, laid-back glamor, cocktails by the beach. It was just what she needed. These last few weeks had left her shaken and anxious, more highly strung than usual, and she needed to decompress.

Ignoring the tension inside the vehicle, she concentrated on replying to queries, ordering samples, and a host of other requests. Her inbox was overflowing. There was never enough time to get through all of them. Thank goodness her assistant took care of the majority, flagging the important or urgent ones that needed her attention.

Half an hour later, they pulled into the VIP parking area at the airport. Viper had made excellent time, but then the roads weren't busy at this hour.

He hauled her two enormous cases out of the trunk, including a beat-up leather duffel bag for himself. Distressed leather would be the correct term, which ironically was trending right now, but she had a sneaky feeling his bag had gotten that way through overuse, not a process in a factory.

Compared to her, he traveled light, but then he wasn't the one hauling and entire range of clothing around.

"I'm going to grab a coffee," she told him after she'd checked her luggage. "Do you want one?"

"I'm good, thanks."

"Okay, suit yourself." Who didn't want coffee at 6 AM?

She walked ahead of him to the Starbucks counter. He stuck to her like glue. So much so, she could almost feel his body heat, or was that her overactive imagination? In her head, she pictured him on a beach, surfboard in hand, dripping wet...

Okay, enough of that!

"Is it necessary to stand so close," she muttered.

"I'm sorry, ma'am, but it's getting busy in here. It would be better if you sat somewhere less crowded."

He did have a point. Anyone in this crowd could be holding a knife or some other weapon. She bought her coffee moved to the executive lounge. Viper's massive shoulders relaxed once they were out of the fray, making her realize he'd been as on edge as she was.

Scanning the room, he said, "This is much better."

"Take a seat." She gestured to the row of chairs next to her and checked her phone again. In the last ten minutes she'd received messages from her assistant, Emily; as well as the ad executive who was meeting her in San Diego with the models and crew; her stylist; and Robert. She sighed and read Robert's message first.

Have a good trip, darling. I'll try to get out there next week.

He ended it with a kiss.

She sighed. He was persistent, if nothing else. They'd only been on a few dates and weren't by any means exclusive, but he always treated her like gold, and she knew it had been her father's wish that they marry. "Robert is a good man, Izzy," he'd told her once. "And he's good for the company. You two would make a formidable team."

Except, that was the problem.

Her father was thinking about the company, not her. It wasn't unusual; he'd been doing that for as long as she could remember. During her formative years, he'd spent more time in Mexico than he had at home. Apart from school vacations at exotic beach resorts, most of her childhood memories were made at boarding school.

Emily messaged again. "I'm here! WTH are you?"

She smiled. What would she do without Emily? Apart from being one of her closest friends, as an assistant, she was worth her weight in gold.

"Exec lounge," she texted back.

A short while later, a petite, cherubic woman with bright eyes and flushed cheeks came bounding in, pulling her cabin case behind her. "There you are!" She hurried over to Izzy.

Viper leaped to his feet and positioned himself between them.

Emily skidded to a halt, looking up at the man who towered over her. "Whoa! Hello. Who is this?" She turned to Izzy, her eyebrows raised.

Izzy couldn't resist a grin. "Emily, meet my bodyguard, Viper. Viper, this is Emily, my assistant."

"Sorry, ma'am." Viper shook her hand and resumed his seat.

Emily gave him an approving look.

"He'll do," she whispered, as she sat down beside Izzy.

Izzy flushed and elbowed her friend in the ribs, hoping Viper hadn't heard. Emily wasn't known for her subtlety.

"I've just gotten a message from Clint," her assistant told her, her gaze still lingering on Viper. "He's been held up in Barcelona, but he said not to worry, he'll be there by this evening."

Izzy paled. "He'd better be. The shoot is tomorrow morning."

"Who's Clint?" Viper asked, his blue eyes slanting. "I don't recall his name on the list you sent me."

She frowned. "Oh, didn't I include him? I meant to. Clint is my stylist. He does my hair and makeup for my social media snaps."

She could see the muscles tighten in his jaw. "Anyone else you forgot to include?"

Izzy glared at him. "I don't think so."

"Is he always this friendly?" Emily whispered.

"Can you be a little less obvious?" hissed Izzy. The last thing she wanted to do was antagonize the guy. He might be an employee, but she had to live with him glued to her heels for the next few weeks.

"Sorry, but he's totally hot. I haven't seen that much raw male energy since we did the lifeguard calendar shoot in Miami last year. Where did you find him?"

Izzy stifled a laugh. "I didn't. My Uncle Pat assigned him to me because of the threatening letters."

"He made a good choice. It's gonna be fun having him around."

"Hands off, Emily," Izzy warned. "He's here to do a job."

"Oh, so you're calling dibs on him, huh?"

"Of course not!" Her cheeks burned. "He's here to protect me. I don't want anything to get in the way of that."

Emily gave her a cheeky grin. "Sure, hun. Whatever you say."

Izzy shook her head. Emily had been her friend since high school and her assistant for the last few years, ever since her online profile had exploded and became too big for her to handle. Emily had gotten a job as a virtual assistant straight out of college, even though she'd studied modern languages at college, so when Izzy had considered bringing someone onboard, she'd looked no further than her friend.

Their flight was called, and they boarded the plane that would take them to San Diego. If Viper was surprised at the first-class seating, he didn't show it. In fact, it was hard to get a reaction out of him at all.

He stowed their cabin cases in the overhead compartments and eased himself into the aisle seat. A solid barrier between them and the rest of the plane.

Izzy couldn't fault his professionalism, but when it came to his social skills, she feared he might be lacking. He was very removed, and still hadn't looked directly at her—not since that accidently glance in the rearview mirror.

She tried to get comfortable beside him, but he was so broad that the slightest movement meant her arm brushed his, or her leg connected with his thigh. Each time, she jolted away, while he didn't budge. Fine. She'd just sit absolutely still, except that didn't work either, so she angled her body away from him to talk to Emily. Who would have thought having a bodyguard would be so stressful?

CHAPTER 5

"Wait here," Viper ordered as they approached the hotel room.

Izzy shot Emily an annoyed glance, but both women complied while he conducted a thorough search of the suite.

The flight had been excruciating, not that he'd even noticed. Izzy had tried to concentrate on the upcoming schedule with Emily, but every time she felt the heat from his rock-hard thigh or a nudge from his marble forearm, she'd tensed up. Eventually, Emily had asked if she was all right. She'd made some excuse about being on edge because of the letters. Now she'd had enough, and all she wanted to do was get changed and relax by the pool.

"Okay, it's clear."

"Thank you." She marched past him into the room. Emily followed, batting her eyelashes.

"Feel free to search mine too," she said coquettishly.

To Izzy's surprise, the corners of his mouth lifted. "It's not part of my job description, ma'am."

"Pity," Emily murmured.

Izzy shot her a warning glance.

"You take the second bedroom, ma'am," Viper told her just as she'd sat down on the bed and kicked off her shoes.

She sighed. "Why?"

"So, if anyone comes looking for you, they have to go through me first."

It was true, the suite consisted of two adjoining rooms and a small lounge with a balcony overlooking a palmed courtyard with a swimming pool and terrace.

Izzy nodded, pushed herself off the bed, and with Emily following, padded through to the adjoining room. Viper followed, wheeling her suitcases through. He set them down in the center of the room. "I'll be next door if you need me."

"Holy crap," muttered Emily, closing the door after him. "He takes his job seriously, doesn't he?"

"I suppose he has to," she allowed. The guy was ex-military, and growing up with an uncle like Pat, she was familiar with that kind of stoic demeanor and uncompromising discipline. It was a thing with them. In a way, she found it reassuring, but in other ways she wished he'd be more human. Crack a joke or make a sarcastic comment. Anything to show he wasn't just a well-trained robot.

What did she care if he was?

To distract herself, Izzy began unpacking her makeup. "What's the agenda for tomorrow?"

"Weren't you listening to a word I said on the plane?" Emily swiped at her tablet. "The crew is arriving at six to set up. Oh, that includes your hair and makeup, by the way. The models are arriving at eight and hopefully, we can get rolling by nine."

"What's the location?" she asked.

"Max wants to shoot them on the beach. Early morning and late afternoon light is best. There's a semi-secluded bay around the corner that won't be too busy. We'll set up there. I was thinking of getting all the beach shots out of the way on

Day 1, with a two-hour break for lunch when the sun is at its hottest. We can do the catalog shots by the hotel pool and in the landscaped gardens over the next two days."

"Sounds good. Make sure the hotel knows the crew can eat and drink here. Put it on my tab."

"Right. Clint is flying in later tonight, so you won't have him this evening, but that's not a train wreck. You're pretty good at doing your own hair now and we won't take any promo shots until tomorrow."

"Good, I want an evening to settle in. I'm thinking, a light dinner at the hotel and then maybe a little stroll around town, just to get the lay of the land. What do you think?"

Emily grinned. "Sounds perfect."

"Right now, however, I'm going for a swim. Did you see that pool as we walked in?" She was dying to wash away the tension of the flight and stretch out her achy muscles.

"Divine. I'll meet you there."

Emily left and Izzy changed into one of her swimsuits. She chose a black one with high sides and a plunging neckline. It made her legs look even longer and emphasized her ample breasts. It was one of her favorites of the entire collection. Very Bond-girl.

She didn't bother with a sarong. One of her mottos was to be proud of what you've got. That's what she tried to portray on her Instagram feed. Don't hide your body away, flaunt it. Everyone is beautiful in their own way. She opened the door to the adjoining room and found Viper standing in his underwear.

Unsure what to do, she froze. "Shit, I'm sorry."

Move! the voice in her head screamed, but she couldn't take her eyes off of him.

A brawny chest with a smattering of dark hair over an intricate military tattoo, bulging arms, and sculpted washboard abs sporting a six-pack—or was it an eight-pack?—she wasn't sure. Her gaze drifted lower. Tight boxers hugged those powerful thighs and beneath, stretching the fabric and leaving little to the imagination, was an impressive bulge. To give him credit, he didn't gasp or reach for a towel, he simply stood there, unfazed.

"Sorry, ma'am. You caught me by surprise. I wasn't expecting you."

Clearly.

She cleared her throat. "My mistake. I'm going down to the pool for a swim. See you there." She made to walk past him, but he shot out an arm, blocking her way.

"I'm sorry, I can't allow that, ma'am. If you'll give me a minute, I'll accompany you."

She paused, trying not to ogle. He was so close, she could reach out and touch that taut, muscly arm. For a crazy moment, she pictured running her hands up it and over his rippling shoulders. Down girl! What the hell had gotten into her? She wasn't usually this… hormonal.

Spinning on her heel, she said, "Okay, I'll wait in my room."

CHAPTER 6

*V*iper sighed in annoyance. Trust her to barge in like she owned the place without so much as a knock. That woman gave no thought to anyone else's privacy but her own. Well, after today, she might think twice about doing that again. She'd certainly flushed redder than a lobster when she'd seen him standing in his boxers. Served her right. Women like Izzy thought the world revolved around them.

But damn if she didn't look good in that swimsuit. More than good. Fucking phenomenal. Those breasts! Full and womanly, spilling over the top of her swimsuit. Jesus, he had to fight not to stare at them. It was all he could do to keep it in his goddamn pants. Thank goodness he'd managed to keep his cool.

He quickly pulled on jeans and a white T-shirt, it would be cooler in the harsh Californian sun. Now that they were at their destination and not in transit, he didn't bother with the vest, or the suit. That would just attract attention. It was unlikely anything would happen here, under the hotel's top-notch security cameras, but you couldn't be too sure. It seemed everyone knew Izzy's itinerary in advance, which meant the threatening letter writer could also be aware of her movements.

When he was ready, he knocked on the connecting door. "Miss Beaumont?"

She opened it, those gorgeous breasts within touching distance, a thin cream-colored sarong tied around her waist.

"I'm ready." She strode past him toward the door. He could see the perfectly rounded globes of her butt through the sheer fabric.

"Wait."

She stopped.

"Stay behind me."

She remained silent as he opened the door and checked the corridor, although he sensed the daggers she was glaring at his back. Tough, there was nothing he could do about that. His job was to keep her safe, and he was following protocol. "Okay."

He gestured for her to follow him.

They walked down the hallway and got into the elevator. She didn't say a word on the way down, simply stared ahead at the steel doors as if praying they would open. When they did, he put out an arm. "Let me go first."

This time she sighed but obliged. Miss Beaumont obviously wasn't used to being told what to do.

Viper surveyed the lobby, the balcony, and the door to the stairwell. As a trained sniper, he knew where to find the vantage points, but they were all clear. He clocked visitors, guests, and staff. Nothing out of the ordinary. He gave a curt nod.

They walked through the lobby, Izzy staying close to him, and out onto the terrace and to the swimming pool. Again, he scanned the guests. It was fairly crowded, but nothing struck him as odd. People were laughing and enjoying them-selves or sunning on loungers.

He scanned the brush around the edge of the pool, the palm trees, and glanced up at the hotel balconies overlooking the courtyard. Clear.

"Darling, over here!" Emily beckoned from a lounge chair. She'd reserved the one beside her for Izzy, while the enormous red, white, and blue sun umbrella in between provided some much-needed shade. "I'm sorry, Viper. I didn't book one for you. Should I have?"

"No, ma'am," he replied. "I'll be standing back here." He took a few steps back.

"Always on guard," Emily mused, turning to Izzy. "So sexy." Izzy's reply was lost as someone dived into the pool with a splash.

He pulled out his sunglasses and slipped them on. It was very bright out here. Light reflected off the swimming pool into his eyes, making him squint. A shooter would use that to his advantage, masking the glint of the rifle scope. He couldn't afford to miss anything.

Izzy unwrapped her sarong and dived into the water. With a laugh, Emily joined her. They swum a few laps, then floated on their backs and chatted. They seemed closer than employer-employee. More like friends.

For all her glamorous ways, Izzy hadn't thought twice about her hair or makeup as she'd dived into the water. It now splayed out around her as she floated, like a dark halo. He tried not to look at the way her skin shimmered beneath the water, at her endless legs, and cinched in waist. The two friends stood in the middle of the pool talking and laughing, and Viper knew he wasn't the only man gawking at her creamy shoulders and bobbing breasts. At least, she couldn't see his eyes.

He was just admiring the way her long dark hair clung

slickly to her back, when somebody shouted, grabbing his attention. He took a step forward, his hand flying to the gun tucked in the back of his jeans, but it was only a boisterous college kid pushing his buddy into the pool.

Shit, his concentration had lapsed for a moment because his focus had been solely on her. Like every other red-blooded man in the place.

"I needed that," Izzy said, emerging dripping from the pool. Christ, did she have any idea what she was doing to him? Idly, she stretched out on the lounge chair. A cat basking in the sun.

"I'm so glad you didn't cancel this trip because of those threats," her assistant said. "It would have been a real shame."

"I'm not going to let some whack-job scare me out of running my business. Besides, I've got Viper now. He'll protect me."

"I'm sure he will," Emily replied, casting a glance over her shoulder at him. Viper didn't mind the assistant's flirtations. He could tell she wasn't serious. It was just a bit of fun. Besides, it helped lighten the mood, which had become very intense on the airplane.

He'd sensed Izzy's stiffness but couldn't work out if it was his presence that bothered her, or the fact that he was invading her space. Either way, he'd been relieved when they'd landed in San Diego.

Izzy was hard to read. She switched between being annoyed with him and sending him intense glances that penetrated like a laser. Having a bodyguard was an inconvenience to her, he got that, but at the same time, he could tell she was anxious about the threats. Whenever someone mentioned them, like now, she coiled up, stiffened her shoulders and jutted out her chin. Classic defense stance.

Oh, yeah. She felt the pressure, even if she tried not to show it.

"Robert's going to fly out too," Izzy said.

"Why don't you sound overjoyed at the prospect?" Emily began applying sunscreen to her fair legs. She didn't have that same olive complexion that Izzy had.

"I was hoping to have a few days to myself."

"Robert's a catch, Izzy," said Emily. "And he adores you. You could do far worse than him."

"What if I don't feel the same way," she murmured, lowering her voice. Viper stared unflinchingly ahead, pretending he couldn't hear. "Robert's a sweetheart, don't get me wrong, but he doesn't stir my blood, you know?"

"You want someone to stir your blood?" Emily stopped what she was doing and looked over at Izzy, who laughed.

"You know what I mean. There's no passion. I don't want to rip his clothes off."

Viper held back a smile.

"You know I'm a great advocate of clothes-ripping passion," Emily told her, grinning. "But, if we're talking life partners, there's a lot more to it than sex. You want someone who'll look after you and treat you right. A friend to take life's journey with."

"I've got enough friends," she remarked.

Emily chortled. "Maybe you'll feel differently when it's just the two of you. This is a very romantic hotel."

"The three of us, you mean." She gave a backward nod.

Emily half-turned. "Oh, yeah. I forgot."

They began talking about the photo shoot after that, so Viper zoned out. An hour later, Izzy went for another swim, while Emily chatted up a group of Spanish-speaking guys who, judging by their bags stuffed with clubs, were on a golfing vacation.

He watched while Izzy frolicked in the water. After a while, she swam to the side and rested her arms on the edge, kicking breaststroke underwater with her legs. The swimsuit had ridden up and her smooth butt cheeks wavered in the water.

He had a fleeting visual of her lying on top of him, his hands clutching those butt cheeks, squeezing them as she slid up and down his… Jesus Christ. Where was his head? He swallowed and forced himself to relax. This was worse than hours of waiting for a target to appear, keeping his breathing even, his arms relaxed, ready to react when the time was right.

"You want to come in?" she called.

"Not while I'm on duty," he replied. What he would give to be able to get in there with her.

Easy, soldier. Breathe. Clear your mind. Relax.

He had to keep his head free of erotic thoughts, otherwise he was doomed. This was an ongoing position, there was no telling when it might end, and he couldn't be lusting after the principal the whole time. It would drive him crazy. It *was* driving him crazy.

"Maybe later, then?" she said. "When you're off duty. You deserve a break."

He was surprised. She'd actually thought of someone else besides herself.

"Thank you, ma'am."

She sighed. "I thought I told you not to call me that."

"Apologies, Miss Beaumont."

She rolled her eyes and pushed away from the side. He watched as she swam a few more leisurely lengths before getting out. Once again, she had a captive audience. Viper resisted the urge to rush over with her sarong to prevent the other men ogling her. The rush of possessiveness surprised him. What did he care if she flaunted her body? She had every right. He was just there to protect it, nothing else.

She lifted a hand, and a hovering waiter came scuttling over. After ordering something, he couldn't hear what, she walked back to her lounge chair, shot him a languid smile, and lay down. Emily had scooted over to where the golfing boys sat and was perched on the end of one of their lounge chairs.

Izzy glance over at her assistant, then pick up her phone. "You can join them if you like, Miss Beaumont."

"That's okay," she replied. "I'm not in the mood for socializing."

Fair enough.

A moment later, the waiter appeared with three mojitos on a tray. She turned around, peering over the lounge chair at him. "I got you a drink."

"I can't while I'm on duty, ma'am, er, Miss Beaumont. But thanks anyway."

She lifted her sunglasses so he could see the mocking look in her eyes. "It's a virgin, Viper. Surely you've had one of those before?"

Boy, did she like to get the upper hand.

CHAPTER 7

*I*zzy left Emily flirting by the pool and went back to her room to lie down and catch up on some emails. Allison, her father's D.C.-based executive assistant, was emailing her meeting schedules and filling her in on operating decisions Robert had made regarding Omega Enterprises.

Thank God for Robert. He'd been effectively running the company for years, since her father preferred to live on site. After his death, she and Robert had flown out to Mexico to meet the site manager, a tough local engineer called Luis Alvarez who was in charge of the miners and the day-to-day workings of the site.

Alvarez was rapidly promoted to General Operations Manager of the Montezuma Project and his remit had expanded to include the distribution network, railroad and port infrastructure, and decision-making powers. They'd spent two weeks helping him build a close-knit team of supervisors, assistants, and security officers to run the mine.

Security was outsourced to an American company operating out of Guatemala, mostly ex-soldiers and mercenaries, not unlike Blackthorn Security. It was necessary, Robert said, to prevent theft and random attacks by banditos and drug barons who wanted a piece of the action.

Omega Enterprises owned and operated several mines across Mexico. These included significant projects in Sonora, Zacatecas, and Guerrero. Each of these operations was profitable and managed by capable local teams. She had met all the managers after her father had passed away, ensuring continuity and a personal touch in the management of their extensive operations.

Robert oversaw all the mines from the D.C. office. He made high-level decisions and effectively ran the company. Her role was more like that of a silent partner, but she still wanted to know what was going on.

"The board was worried that I'd sell my share of the company after my father died," she told Viper on the way up to the suite. She had no idea why she was sharing with him other than he was a great listener—probably because he didn't say much, and she needed to off-load. "To be honest, I thought about it, but the company meant so much to him that I decided to keep things as they were. Not rock the boat too much, so to speak. As it was, we lost market share when my father died."

"I can imagine," Viper said, politely.

She sighed. "Anyway, it's left me with a lot of extra work, not that I'm involved in the day-to-day running of the company. That's Robert's job." She glanced across at him. "Robert Hampton-Barnes was my father's Chief Financial Officer, but I've promoted him to CEO. You'll meet him next week if he manages to get out here for a few days."

Okay, so she was babbling, but Viper simply let her carry on, nodding in all the appropriate places. It felt good to air her thoughts, even if she wasn't getting a response. She couldn't discuss such things with Emily, who was a genius when it came to fashion and marketing, not so much running a corporation.

"I like to keep tabs on what's going on. Allison, that's my father's, now Robert's exec assistant, keeps me abreast of any new developments."

Another wordless nod. They walked down the corridor to their suite. She stood back while Viper opened the door—see, she was learning—and checked the adjoining rooms before allowing her entry. "All clear, Miss Beaumont."

She glanced up at him, exasperated. "Izzy, please."

"I feel more comfortable with Miss Beaumont, ma'am, if you don't mind."

"Whatever." Would it hurt him so much to relax a little? She didn't bite. He hadn't even flinched when she'd barged in on him in his underwear. Not a flicker. She was beginning to wonder if he possessed any emotions at all.

"I'm going to my room. We'll be heading out around seven, but order room service if you're hungry," she told him, aware he hadn't had lunch. "Charge it to the room."

"Thank you," he replied, giving a stiff nod. She wondered where he'd gotten that cut on the side of his head. Must be recent. It looked like there were still a couple of stitches in it. Another assignment, maybe? Had he fended off an attack on another vulnerable victim?

She swallowed, suddenly weary. The constant tension was beginning to weight on her. Conversely, Viper appeared calm and collected, but then he always did. A sniper, patiently waiting for a chance to strike. Was that how he'd gotten his nickname? He saw her studying him. "Was there something else, Miss Beaumont?"

"No, but I'll be quite safe in the suite, if you want to take some time to yourself."

"I'm good, thank you."

She gave a tight nod. "Suit yourself."

. . .

IT WAS A BEAUTIFUL BALMY EVENING. Not a breath of air and the heat from the day encased the city in a warm glow, as if it were still basking in the residual warmth of the sun.

"Wow, that's breathtaking," gasped Emily, staring out over the Pacific Ocean that mirrored the pink, peach, and yellow of the changing sky. Izzy had to admit, it was stunning. Viper was wearing those aviator sunglasses he'd worn by the pool, so she couldn't tell if he was looking at the sunset or not.

Emily had wanted to go out for a drink, so she'd agreed, even though she hadn't really been in the mood. *Snap out of it,* she told herself sternly, glancing at Viper walking next to her. To the casual observer, he could be mistaken for her boyfriend. Taller than both of them, arms bulging out of that shirt, hotter than hell with his square jaw covered with stubble. Impossible to ignore. It was a stunning evening, they were on a working vacation, and she was lucky to be here. Why was she letting a few poison pen letters get the better of her?

So far, nothing had come of them. They'd been idle threats. It was Pat who had convinced her to take them seriously. Pat who'd insisted they assign her a close protection officer for the next few weeks, just until the cops could get to the bottom of who was sending them.

He might seem casual, but she knew him well enough to know he was on full alert. She felt the concentration radiating off him like a ball of wound-up electricity, waiting to be unleashed.

Just ignore him, Pat had said. *He'll stay in the background. You won't even know he's there.*

Ha! Fat chance.

Sure, he really blended into the background.

The way he watched her was unsettling too. Watched

without seeing, if that made any sense. No direct eye contact, but she was never out of his sight.

If she were brutally honest, it was also damn sexy. She found herself doing things for his benefit. Lounging in front of him, tilting her head at just the right angle, flaunting her body. She knew how to show herself off to her best advantage, and she was turning it on, just for him.

This evening she'd picked this particular outfit because she'd thought he'd like it. How crazy was that? He was nobody. So why was he demanding so much of her attention, without even trying?

"How do I look?" she'd asked him before they'd left the suite, doing a little pirouette in the hotel room.

"Very nice, ma'am."

Nice?

That's the best he could do? *Nice* didn't get her thousands of likes and comments online. *Nice* didn't grow her following or get her contracts with top brands. To make matters worse, he hadn't even looked at her when he'd said it.

"You're not yourself tonight," Emily remarked, as they browsed the lit-up designer stores, tourist shops, bars, and restaurants in the town. "You're very quiet. Is something wrong?"

"No, just thinking about the shoot tomorrow," she replied.

She definitely wasn't sulking.

Nice, indeed.

"Ooh, look at this fabulous jewelry." Emily grabbed her hand and dragged her into a glamorous store with shiny, well-lit cabinets filled with sparkling trinkets. She saw Viper frown, then follow them in. He stood patiently at the door, while she browsed with Emily, finally picking out a silver chain with a lovely turquoise pendant on it.

"I want to wear it," she announced, turning to Viper. "Won't you put it on for me?"

He hesitated, then nodded.

She gave it to him and turned around, lifting her hair. To her surprise, he deftly opened the clasp and hung it over her head, brushing her arm with his. She shivered, as his fingers secured it at the nape of her neck. He didn't fumble once, not even with those big, callused hands of his.

"You've done that before." She shot him a slanting look. He didn't react.

"Dexterous too," winked Emily, walking past.

They moved on to a restaurant where they sat outside and ordered shellfish and a bottle of wine. To be fair, Viper stood several meters away giving them some space while they ate, but he was constantly on guard. She could tell by the way he kept looking up and down the street. He'd removed his sunglasses now that the sun had set, but he still didn't look at her. Not once.

What the hell did she have to do to get his attention, and why the hell did she care?

They passed a popular bar with loud music and a crowd spilling out onto the sidewalk. Everyone was laughing and drinking and dancing to the beats, created by a DJ inside the bar.

"Let's have a dance," Emily said, pulling Izzy inside. Viper shouldered his way in after them.

"This is not the safest place for you to be, Miss Beaumont," he shouted, raising his voice to be heard over the noise. "I can't protect you in a place like this."

"I like it here," she retorted, fed up with being scared, fed up with not getting a reaction out of him, and needing to let her hair down. The revelers were shoulder to shoulder, some lounging, some gyrating, everybody having a good time.

"Let's dance." Emily pulled her onto the dance floor. "Come on, Viper. Have some fun." He scowled after them, but didn't move, preferring to stay by the bar where he could watch her from afar. With his six-foot-something height, he looked over most people's heads.

It took all of five minutes before Izzy and Emily were besieged by man wanting to join them. Izzy ignored them, absorbing the music, enjoying the sensation of letting go. One of the men shouted something inaudible in her ear. She ignored him, and glanced up at Viper, who was staring straight at her, an intense look on his face.

Now he looks at me.

She beckoned, but he didn't budge. Didn't move. Simply stood there, glaring at her.

Fine. Be like that.

In a moment of rebellion, she turned it up a notch, bringing out all her hottest moves. The circle of predatory men around them deepened. But every time she looked up she saw his gaze fixed on her above their heads. Unblinking. Unsmiling.

She danced on, losing herself in the music. The DJ was on fire. Lasers shot multi-colored beams across the club. Artificial smoke billowed out from vents at floor level.

One of the men grabbed her arm and pulled her against him. She wouldn't normally have minded, except he was groping her ass and grinding his pelvis against hers. She tried to push him away, but he wouldn't budge.

"You're so sexy," he murmured hotly in her ear. She could smell the alcohol on his breath, even above the smoke.

"Get off me." She pushed against his chest.

"What's the matter, sweetheart? I saw the way you were looking at me."

Bullshit.

She'd been looking at *him.*

She tried to wriggle free, but he gripped her harder. She sighed, used to these sorts of situations. He wasn't a threat, simply an inebriated oaf who didn't know when to quit. She'd dance some more, then slide out of his grip.

Except she didn't get the chance. A shadow loomed behind them and before she could gasp, her dance partner went careening backwards into another group of dancers.

"The lady said get off," a voice growled.

"Hey!" The drunk guy took a step forward, saw the look on Viper's face, and the size of him, and held up his hands. "Sorry, man. Didn't know she was taken."

Viper.

He grabbed her hand and pulled her out of the club. Emily was still molded to some guy with long hair and a leather thong around his neck. They'd just gotten outside when she turned on him.

"What do you think you're doing?"

"What I'm paid to do."

"I can look after myself. That sort of thing happens all the time."

He stared stonily ahead.

A bouncer hurried over. "Everything all right?" He eyed Viper up and down. Unlike the drunk guy, he knew a formidable opponent when he saw one.

"Personal security." Viper flashed a card in the bouncer's face.

Izzy nodded. "He's mine. We're good."

The bouncer nodded and disappeared back into the club.

"I don't need you fighting my battles for me," Izzy continued, feeling her suppressed annoyance come flooding back.

"That's what I'm paid to do."

"Not on the dance floor," she retorted. "It was hardly an assassination attempt."

"You looked like you were struggling. I was just doing my job."

"Okay, well can we limit your involvement to real danger like kidnappings and attempts on my life from now on?"

"I'm afraid not, Miss Beaumont. If I see you're in trouble, I'm going to step in."

She rolled her eyes. "Okay, Mr. Macho. I get it. I can see I'm not going to be having much fun with you around."

"I'm sorry about that, ma'am."

She huffed, resisting the urge to pummel his chest. This man made her so mad. "We may as well go back to the hotel. And for God's sake, stop calling me ma'am."

CHAPTER 8

$\mathcal{H}$e was in trouble.

Viper walked along the sidewalk to their hotel, Izzy a step behind him.

Hell, *she* was trouble.

Watching her dance, he'd felt things he hadn't felt in a long time. Feelings that weren't particularly welcome. Possessiveness, lust, jealousy. He'd wanted to beat that drunk guy to a pulp for grabbing her like that. For holding her beautiful body against his uncouth, sweaty one. For gripping her butt like it was his property.

Idiot.

Except he couldn't do that, obviously. Not on duty. Not now he had a reason for getting up in the morning. Blade had given him a purpose, a shot at a real job, one he actually wanted. He was going to do his best to keep this job, no matter what.

Bar fights and drinking away the boredom were a thing of the past.

They got to the hotel, walked through the lobby and up

the elevator in silence. He sensed her silently fuming beside him. She was mad at him. He got it.

She was used to living her own life, on her own terms. Having a PPO was a new experience for her. Lots of the principals he'd guarded had been the same at first, but they got used to it. And in South American, where he'd spent the last few months before he'd been shot, protection was a serious business. Foreign diplomats, engineers, and executives were kidnapped all the time. Sometimes not even for ransom, but to make a point. Their deaths were a macabre message to the American conglomerates.

Stay out of our country. You don't belong here.

But in the end, money talked, and the corporations kept sending personnel, which meant there was always work for the likes of him.

A packed beach bar in San Diego was a different type of war zone—one he wasn't familiar with. But the rules were the same. Protect the principal at all costs. From whatever threat presented itself, be it a rooftop sniper or a drunk man on a dance floor. One thing he was not going to do was apologize for doing his job. She'd just have to deal with it until the threat on her life was neutralized. This was her new reality.

He unlocked the door using the keycard, then took a quick look around. "It's clear."

Izzy stomped in behind him.

"Will Emily be okay?" he asked, aware they'd left her on the dancefloor at the mercy of those men.

"Yeah, she'll be fine. Emily is remarkably resourceful," she said, walking past him to her room. "She'll find her way back to the hotel. Don't worry about her." He got the feeling this was the way their nights ended more often than not.

"I'm sorry if I ruined your evening," he said bluntly.

She turned around, her arms crossed in front of her like

she was hugging herself. "It's okay. I shouldn't have put you in that position."

There was a heavy pause where they just looked at each other. Eventually, he gave a tight nod. "Good night, Miss Beaumont."

"Goodnight, Viper."

He waited until he heard the lock in her door turn, before he sat down on the bed.

Viper had fought and survived in places of unimaginable chaos, but the swimsuit fashion shoot nearly undid him. Twelve demanding models, all requiring makeup, hair, styling, and ego flattering. Eleven different locations on the beach, behind rocks, in the water, beyond the crashing breakers, and on the sandy beach. Ten crew members carrying everything from giant white umbrella screens and lighting to heavy-duty camera stands and props. It was like a bad freaking Christmas song.

And Izzy was everywhere at once.

He watched her flit from prepping the models and guiding the stylist, to talking to the photographer and advising the art director. Emily was there too in an enormous pair of tortoiseshell sunglasses, armed with a clipboard, her phone glued to her ear. He wondered what time she'd gotten back last night.

He had to give Izzy credit, she knew exactly what she wanted. The models had to pose in a natural way, doing things normal women did. Running, swimming, jumping, playing bat and ball, frolicking through the waves. There were even a few male models for complementary shots. Walking along the beach holding hands, kissing in the water, throwing a frisbee to each other.

It was very well organized. Izzy wanted the photographer

to capture real-life moments and from what Viper could see, he did what he was told, only pausing to yell, "Show me your cleavage, darling!" or "I know it's sunny, but open your eyes!" or "Too much glow. Can we take it down a notch?"

He also took some shots of Izzy. Poses that made Viper's mouth go dry. Izzy kneeling in the shallows, her head back, laughing. Izzy lying on the dry sand, grains caked on her breasts and in her hair. Izzy lounging against a rock, her hips thrust forward evocatively.

Her personal stylist, Clint, had spent the better part of the morning in her suite doing her hair and makeup, and casting unashamedly hot glances in his direction. Izzy had been transformed into an even more beautiful version of herself, if that was possible, with perfect makeup, a shimmering golden glow, and glossy lips that begged to be kissed.

Viper had vetted the advertising company, but it was impossible to check out the individual crew members, many of whom were freelancers, so he'd spent the entire day performing risk assessments, ruling out potential threats, and shadowing her every move.

She kept going, barely stopping for lunch, guiding and supervising her team, and looking more beautiful and glamorous than the models themselves. Her energy was boundless, he didn't know how she did it. The sun was sinking over the sea when she finally called it quits for the day.

Everybody heaved a collective sigh of relief.

"We'll start at first light tomorrow," she called, as the exhausted crew packed up and the models sauntered back to their hotel rooms to rest and recuperate.

"That was a good day, Viper," she said, as he helped her carry cases of swimsuits and accessories up to her room.

"That's great, ma'am."

"I think we got some really good shots. Max is going to send the proofs to me this evening." Her cheeks were pink from the sun, and she had sand stuck in her eyelashes and on her chest. Her hair was disheveled, held back by a pair of enormous sunglasses, and the slip dress she wore over her bikini had fallen off one golden shoulder. His heart skipped a beat as she smiled up at him.

Fuck, he was smitten.

"Did you enjoy yourself?" she asked.

"I'm not sure if enjoy is the right word," he replied. "It was interesting. I've never been on a fashion shoot before." It was very different from his brand of chaos.

"I could tell." She smiled again and he wondered what she meant. Had he looked that out of place? "It can be frantic, but this crew is very professional. I've used them countless times before. They know how I work."

"At the pace of an Indy 500 race?"

She laughed. "Something like that."

Not once had she mentioned last night, which he was relieved about. They seemed to have reached a tentative truce. He checked the suite and let her in.

"I'm going to take a shower," she said, pausing at the door to her room. "Then I've got some work to do."

"Don't you ever take a break?" The words were out before he could stop himself.

She grinned. "I'm a workaholic, hadn't you noticed?"

He snorted.

"Anyway, it's follow-up stuff. Usually, I don't mind, I love what I do, but lately, with father's death and the drama around that, I've been feeling a little burned out. That's why I wanted a few days here by myself after the shoot." Her shoulders dropped. "But now Robert's coming."

Robert, the man who's clothes she did not want to rip off. "Is that a bad thing?"

"It is when you want peace and quiet. He'll insist on

talking about the company and while that is important, it's not what I need right now."

Viper didn't reply. It wasn't his place to suggest that she tell Robert not to come, to put up some boundaries, even if that's what he was thinking. Hell, he didn't want Robert Hampton-Whatshisname anywhere near her.

Her phone rang. "Excuse me."

She answered it as she went through the connecting door into her suite. "Hi, Max. Great job today." Viper left her to it. She hadn't closed the door behind her so he could hear her chatting on the phone while he took off his shirt. Damn, that felt good.

After locking the suite door from the inside, he walked into the bathroom and turned on the shower. He also needed to get rid of the sand and sweat that had accumulated during the day.

He was about to strip off his jeans, when he glanced at the open interleading door. Izzy was still talking on the phone, unaware she'd left it open. Not wanting to risk a repeat of yesterday's interruption, he grabbed a fresh set of clothes and took them into the bathroom with him. A moment later he was standing under the cool water, letting it wash away the remnants of the day. Bliss.

Then he heard her voice.

Shit, it sounded like she was in the bathroom.

"Viper? Sorry to interrupt, but Emily's here to go through the schedule for tomorrow. I'm going to let her in, okay?"

"No," he called. "Give me a second."

Bad timing.

He climbed out of the shower, leaving it running, and wrapped a towel around his waist. "Never open the door yourself," he told her, reaching for his gun that was lying on his jeans on the toilet seat. "Don't even look through the peephole. I've seen people get their faces blown off doing that."

"Jesus," she whispered, backing out of the bathroom.

He followed. "Sorry, I didn't mean to frighten you. It's just a precaution."

Striding across to the door, he stood to one side and called out. "Who is it?"

"It's Emily. Viper, let me in."

He opened the door, but not before checking she was alone.

"You took your time," Emily ducked underneath his arm. She looked remarkably well considering her late night and the full day on the beach. Her gaze raked over his glistening body, lingering on his tattoo, then flickered to Izzy whose hair was also damp and combed back off her face. "Did I interrupt something?"

"Don't be silly," Izzy scoffed. "Viper insists on opening the door to everyone, even when he's in the shower. Come in." They disappeared into her suite.

"Were you in the shower with him?" Emily hissed, before the door closed.

Izzy's voice. "Don't be ridiculous."

"Why the fuck not?"

With a sigh, Viper got back into the shower.

CHAPTER 9

"Honey, if his room was this close to mine, I wouldn't come out for anything," Emily said, grinning.

"It's not like that, Em. He's my bodyguard."

"But look at him! He's a freaking god. How can you not be attracted to that?"

"I didn't say I wasn't attracted to him, just that it's not like that between us. He's got a job to do. This is serious."

"So? Can't he protect you during the day and offer you his body at night? It seems only fair?"

Izzy gave up and laughed. "You're impossible. What happened to you last night?"

"Oh, those guys I met by the pool turned up. I ended up spending the night with Matt. He's the cute one with the floppy hair and dimples."

"I thought as much. Sorry I left so early. Viper made things awkward."

"I saw. He sent that guy flying. If that wasn't a manly show of possessiveness, I don't know what is?"

"No way." Izzy shook her head. "He was just doing his job. That guy was harassing me. He wouldn't let me go."

"I've seen you get out of worse situations before," she scoffed. "Are you sure you weren't putting it on just a little to get a reaction out of him?"

"Of course not." Izzy kept her voice steady.

"I know you, Iz. That guy wasn't a threat. Not really."

Izzy sighed. "Let's get back to the schedule, shall we? There's a lot to go over. Tomorrow we have to do the catalog shots."

"Okay, fine, but this conversation is not over." Emily got back to business. "I've reserved the pool for two hours from eight to ten, but after that the hotel wants it for the guests, so we can't waste any time. The gardens are an option, though."

"That's understandable." Izzy pursed her lips, thinking about their options. "We should be able to get at least half of the pool shots done. We can finish the rest on Wednesday."

Izzy couldn't get the image of Viper in his towel out of her mind. His gorgeous, sculpted body had been dripping wet, his hair standing upright, glistening with water. Emily was right, he was a god. Neptune. With eyes the color of the sea.

And she hadn't been laid in over a year.

After Emily left, she lay back on the bed and closed her eyes, loosing herself to a private fantasy.

Viper coming into her room, wet from the shower. He was moving toward the bed, his towel falling aside. Izzy... his voice was low, deep and throaty. Yes, she whispered back, her heart pounding in her chest. He bent over the bed to kiss her, pulling her into his arms. Their lips met. Locking in a hard embrace. Desire made her cling to him, losing herself in that kiss.

Groaning softly, she snaked a hand into her panties.

"Miss Beaumont?" His voice again, but this time it was real.

A knock on the door.

She gasped and sat up, hastily pulling down her dress. "Yes?"

The door opened and his dark head popped round. "I'm going to order something to eat. You want me to get you something?"

She was hungry, but not for food.

Heart racing, she forced herself to concentrate on what he was saying, rather than the way he was making her feel. How easy would it be to go to him, take him by the hand and lead him into the bedroom?

Would he come?

Somehow, she doubted it. Still, it didn't mean a girl couldn't dream.

"Sure, thanks."

"Any preferences?"

"I'll have the burger and fries."

Was that a tiny smile? His eyes crinkled and she saw the faintest hint of a dimple in his right cheek. "Got it."

He disappeared again.

Shaken, she stared after him.

Jumping up, she picked up her laptop and followed him into his bedroom where he was standing by the desk phone. For some reason, she didn't want to be alone. Actually, that wasn't it. She wanted to be around him. Was that weird? Maybe not, given her sexy daydream.

He turned as she walked in, placing a hand over the receiver. "Did you want to order something else?"

She shook her head and sat down at the small table in the corner of his room to wait until he'd finished. "Do you mind if I ask your opinion on something?" she said, the moment he hung up.

He frowned but walked over to her. "Um, sure, although I'm not sure how much help I'll be."

"It's not about fashion."

"It's not?"

"Nope. It's about the way my father died."

"Oh?" He strode over and after a moment's hesitation, took a seat beside her at the table. She could smell his after-shave, the same one she'd noticed in the car. He looked good, fresh from his shower, in beige thigh-hugging chinos and a fitted, white T-shirt. It was impossible to ignore the way his arms bulged from beneath the cotton. The guy was seriously jacked. For a fleeting moment, she imagined those muscular arms wrapped around her, drawing her toward him, and her stomach fluttered.

Come on, Izzy. Concentrate.

Something about the police report had bothered her from the start, and it would help to run it by someone impartial, someone whose profession meant that he'd understand her concern.

"This is the incident report on my father's accident. Would you mind reading it and telling me what you think?"

He narrowed his eyes. "I don't know the specific circum-stances surrounding your father's death, only that he died in a car accident."

She gave a tight nod. "It's all here."

The document was open on the screen, and he read: *OFFICIAL – MEXICAN POLICE* in a bold font across the top.

Izzy turned the screen toward him. "It's been translated, which is why the English isn't that good, but you'll get the gist of it."

He leaned forward and began to read. She watched as his eyes scrolled the page. He read fast, occasionally going back over a line that didn't make sense. The translation was sketchy, but it was easy enough to understand.

Eventually, he looked up. "It's pretty vague on the actual

details, but it sounds to me like he lost control of the vehicle and drove over the edge of a cliff."

"My father grew up in Mexico," Izzy said thoughtfully. "It's always bothered me that he'd lose control like that. He knew those roads backwards, drove them every day. I can't see how he'd simply drive over the edge."

"Do you suspect foul play?" Viper's voice deepened.

"I don't know. Maybe? I mean, think about it. My father dies and his share of the company passes to me. Ordinarily, a woman in my position would sell those shares. I mean, what do I know about running a mining conglomerate, right? I'm into fashion. I have my own company to run. Then, when I decide not to sell, I start getting death threats."

"You think someone is trying to force you to sell the company?"

"It's a possibility, isn't it? I mean, it makes sense. Take out my father, and then go after me."

"You're saying you think he was murdered?"

She shrugged.

"Who would want to do that?" Viper stared at her, suddenly serious. The sea-blue gaze darkened. "Who would benefit if you were gone?"

"That's the problem. I don't know. None of the other board members can afford to buy me out. My father owned half of the company. That's a sizable chunk by anyone's estimate."

"What about his competitors?"

"I've had offers from two other firms. Both operate in Central America. Neither of them was particularly aggressive, though, and I didn't detect any malice in their offers." She sighed. "Do you think I'm crazy?"

"No, of course not. Like you said, it makes sense. You are getting threatening messages to sell the mine."

"That's it!" She snapped her fingers.

"What?"

"I've just realized what was bugging me. The threats only mentioned one of the mines, but we own and operate several in Mexico. Why would they just be concerned with that particular mine?"

He frowned. "You might be onto something there. The letters mentioned Montezuma."

She glanced at him in surprise. "You know the name of the mine?"

"It was in your file."

She pursed her lips. "Good memory."

He didn't reply.

"There's a couple of things I want to look into," she said, thinking out loud.

They were interrupted by a knock on the door.

"Hold that thought." Viper grabbed his gun off the sideboard and answered the door.

It was only room service, and he wheeled in a trolley containing the burgers and fries and two beers. "I didn't know if you wanted one."

"I'd love one."

He opened it for her with a bottle opener from the trolley. A flick of his powerful wrists. She took a long gulp. He transferred the plates to the table, then took a beer and sat back down. "You were saying?"

"I want to talk to the police directly and find out if my father's car was tampered with. I didn't see any report on the car wreck itself."

"It's probably still lying at the bottom of the cliff," Viper said, frowning. "Depending on its position, the local police may not have the capability to retrieve it or get it analyzed."

She bit her lip. "How am I going to find out if this was an accident or not?"

"You could send an investigator to take a look at the

scene," Viper suggested. "A skilled crash analyst can reconstruct the sequence of events based on skid marks, debris patterns, and impact points. They can work out the vehicle's speed and trajectory, try to piece together what happened. They might even be able to tell if the crash was due to a mechanical failure, or the car was tampered with or driven off the road."

"Yes." She regarded him over her burger. It had been the right decision to talk to him about it. "I'll do that."

He watched as she took a bit, then said, "You might also want to speak to the people who worked with your father. They might know if anyone had a reason to want him dead."

She chewed slowly. "If I called my father's head of security, would you talk to him for me?"

Viper paused, clearly unsure.

"Please, you'll know what to say." She hesitated. "And they'll take you more seriously than me."

"Why? You're the owner of the company."

"I'm also a woman." She sighed and gave a reluctant shrug. "It's just the way it is." She knew all too well how easy it was for important men to put her off until mañana, to postpone that meeting, to think that she could be sidelined until later. It had happened a lot since her father had died. An unknown number would be more likely to get the head of security's attention. Sadly.

He fixed his gaze on her. "If that's what you want."

"It is. I've got his telephone number in my contacts somewhere. Maybe you can give him a call now?"

"Now?" He glanced at his watch.

"Yeah, it's not that late." She looked up the number from an email. "His name is Miguel Hernández. Use your phone, that way he won't know it's me calling."

"If you're sure?"

"I am."

He picked up his phone and dialed, moving away from the table. She noticed he liked to pace when he was on the phone.

After a few rings, he said, "Good Evening, my name is Viper Morgan and I'm calling on behalf of Isabella Beaumont."

She smiled at his use of her full name. Hardly anyone called her that anymore.

"I'd like to talk to you about some security concerns involving Mr. Beaumont's death."

A pause.

"Did you visit the site of the accident, Mr. Hernández?"

"Speaker," Izzy mouthed.

Viper put it on speakerphone.

"... gave the police my statement. It appears Mr. Beaumont drove off the road into the ravine."

"Yes, we read the police report," Viper said. "It was a little vague on the details. Could you fill us in? Did a traffic investigator analyze the scene, and if so, where is that report?"

Another pause.

"We don't have anything like that down here. The police services are basic, at best."

"I understand. That's why I'm calling you, Mr. Hernández. As a security expert, I'm sure you had an opinion. I'd like to hear it."

Izzy was impressed. He was confident and had already gotten the man on his side by appealing to his ego.

"Well, I don't want to speak out of turn," he said.

"Please, we value your input. That's why Miss Beaumont asked me to call you."

"All right, look. There were a few things that don't add up," Hernández said. "First, the skid marks. They started abruptly and were at an angle, suggesting Mr. Beaumont swerved suddenly. This doesn't fit with someone who knew the road well."

"I knew it," hissed Izzy.

Viper held up a hand. "Anything else?"

Hernández was warming up now. "There were two sets of tire marks. One matches Mr. Beaumont's car, but the other shows a vehicle accelerating away from the scene, not braking as you'd expect if someone witnessed an accident."

"Opposing marks?" Viper asked.

"Yeah, and we also found some debris scattered along the road leading up to where he went over. Broken glass and plastic, that didn't match his vehicle."

"Have you checked his vehicle?"

A scoff. "No, and we're not likely to either. The vehicle is not accessible with the resources we have here."

Izzy sighed. Darn.

"Why didn't you mention this to the police?" If he had, it would have been in the report.

Another laugh. "I tried, but they seemed uninterested in pursuing it further. They were quick to rule it an accident."

Less work, Izzy guessed.

Viper wasn't done. "One last question."

"Yeah?"

"What's the situation like down there? Are there any rebel groups or local militia who wanted Beaumont gone?"

"You talk like you know the region?" It was a question.

"I've done a few ops down there. U.S. Navy." She noticed he didn't say what he'd done in the Navy.

Still, the tone of Hernández's voice changed. Respect now echoed down the line.

"I was a sergeant in the Mexican Army. To answer your question, La Sombra Roja controls the region, and they want to take over the running of the mine."

"A cartel?" Viper frowned.

"Yeah, my men fend of attacks every few months by gangs affiliated to the cartel. The mine is profitable, it's a good way to legitimize their business." He didn't have to explain. The cartel wanted to use the Montezuma mine to launder their drug money.

"They want to buy the mine?"

"They want to drive it into the ground and then buy it on the cheap. Attacks are bad for business. Employees leave and go elsewhere, investors back out."

Viper grasped what he was saying. "They thought if they abducted the boss, they could ransom her for the mine?"

"That's my guess, but it wouldn't be good for the surrounding communities or the people who work in the mine. La Sombra Roja would run it into the ground, the knock-on effect would be catastrophic."

Izzy felt sick. This was what she'd feared. Without her father, the mine was vulnerable. Without her, it was as good as finished. That's why she hadn't sold and why she held on to her shares, even though she had no interest in running the company herself.

"Okay, we appreciate the feedback. Let us know if you need anything," Viper was saying. "Miss Beaumont wants to help."

"Will do."

Izzy let out a shaky breath, then dropped her head in her hands.

CHAPTER 10

This was bad.

Viper wasn't familiar with La Sombra Roja, but generally speaking, cartel members were a ruthless bunch. Izzy could be in real danger.

"Your father's death does sound suspicious." His voice was low, almost a murmur, as he sat down across from her. "You have a right to be concerned."

Izzy's eyes flashed. "I won't sell, no matter what the threat to me. You heard what Hernández said. The mine is vulnerable. Selling it could lead to people losing their jobs, the work drying up."

Viper nodded. She was brave, but then he wasn't surprised. You didn't get to where she'd gotten without having a good deal of backbone.

"I need to update Pat." He raked a hand through his hair. "If your father was murdered, it makes your situation more precarious. The U.S. authorities should be notified."

Izzy heaved a frustrated sigh. "The FBI know about the threats," she said flatly. "But until an actual crime has been committed, there's not much they can do. They can't get involved in the Mexican side of things."

"They can look into your father's death." Viper leaned forward to make his point. "Although the Mexican police have jurisdiction, the FBI can assist when the crime involves an American citizen."

"Do you think they would?" She stared up at him.

"I'll get Pat to check on that too. He's pretty well connected. I'm sure he can get them involved."

She nodded, a hint of hope flickering in her eyes. "Okay, if you think it'll help."

"In the meantime, I strongly suggest you don't go out more than necessary. Here, at the hotel, I can guard you, but out there in bars and clubs, it's a lot harder."

Izzy sighed again, this time more heavily. "You're right. I need to take this seriously."

Viper hesitated, then asked, "I'm sorry to ask this, but could anyone in the company be sending you these letters? Who benefits if you sold your share?"

Izzy's expression turned dismal. "I thought about that," she admitted. "Robert and Rafael have a few shares, but then so do a lot of other people. Nobody has the money to buy me out. I wish they did."

"What happens if you sold your share to another company?"

"Then that company would have the controlling interest. Robert and Raff would lose their jobs, or if they were kept on, would answer to a new boss. As it stands now, they pretty much run the company. It's in their best interests to keep me here."

Viper nodded slowly. He was beginning to understand the complexity of the situation. "I see."

Her eyes widened. "What Hernández said about the

cartels was frightening. If they got control of the mines, they'd pilfer the profits and run it into the ground or use it to launder their drug money. My father warned me about them."

Viper's face darkened. "It's a high-risk region, particularly for an American."

"It is," Izzy agreed. "But the investment and infrastructure are so good for the local economy and the communities that live there, that my father considered it worth it. He was a courageous man."

Like his daughter.

"When my father acquired the mining rights, the government was promoting industrial growth and foreign investment. He saw an opportunity to make a difference."

Viper's eyes narrowed as he considered the implications. "How would anyone from La Sombra Roja know where to find you?"

"It's easy enough to figure out someone's address," she said.

"True, although the threatening letters were sent from a U.S. location."

"The cartel could have contacts in the United States. Just because the letters weren't sent from Mexico, doesn't mean they wasn't from them."

Viper shook his head, frustrated. "I wish we had more clarity. An unseen enemy is the worst kind. You don't know what you're dealing with."

He felt so damn helpless. Her life was at stake, and the situation had just escalated beyond levels he was comfortable with. He didn't even think Izzy realized just how much danger she could be in.

He glanced down at his burger, which all of a sudden didn't seem nearly so appetizing. This was way more serious than he'd first thought. The threats weren't coming from some obsessed fan or lustful admirer, these guys were organized criminals who wanted her to sell her father's company, and if he knew anything about the cartels, it was that they didn't stop until they'd gotten what they wanted. Even if it meant taking someone's life to do it.

VIPER CALLED Pat as soon as they finished eating. He knew the hardy former Commander wouldn't mind the late hour. Not if it was work-related. To his surprise, Izzy opened her laptop and started working, content to remain in his room. Every now and then she'd smile, shake her head, or raise her eyebrows.

He liked having her here, even though it meant he had to be on his best behavior. Her presence seemed to fill the room, or maybe that was because her fragrant, floral scent kept wafting over to him, tantalizing his senses and sending unwanted thoughts flying through his mind.

"That your signature fragrance?" he asked, taking out his phone to call Pat.

A smile lit up her face. "Yes, do you like it?"

"It suits you." Fresh, uplifting, with a sensual undertone that he found alluring.

"Thanks, I thought so too." Shit, when she smiled at him like that... he'd slay dragons for her. Hell, he might have to.

Pat was understandably concerned after Viper had filled him in on what Hernández had told them about her father's accident, the cartel, and their plan to devalue the enterprise in order to purchase it.

"There's a possibility Beaumont was murdered, sir," Viper said carefully. "In which case—"

"In which case, Izzy's in more danger than we thought."

"Yes, sir."

She kept working, although she'd stopped typing and was gazing at the screen, her finger idly clicking through images.

"I think it's time we escalated this. I'll talk to my contacts in Washington."

"Any news from the police on the letters?" Viper asked.

"Not yet. Fingerprint analysis didn't turn up anything and we're still waiting on the DNA results, but I wouldn't hold my breath."

"Understood, sir."

"How is our girl?"

"She's doing good, sir. She's right here if you'd like to have a word?"

"She's with you now?" He heard the surprise in his boss's voice. It was late—going on midnight. Pat would have assumed Izzy would be fast asleep in her own room by now.

"Um, yeah. We've been discussing the situation in Mexico."

"Put me on."

Viper handed Izzy the phone. She shot him a reassuring smile before she turned her focus on the call. "Uncle Pat, it's good of you to check up on me. Yes, I'm absolutely fine. Viper's doing an awesome job. He literally doesn't let me out of his sight."

Viper tensed, as he felt her gaze wander back to him, but he purposely didn't look up.

"Don't worry, I won't take any risks. He's already given me a stern talking to. Of course I will. Take care. Bye." She handed the phone back with a smug little grin.

"Thank you." He slid it into his pocket. "You didn't have to sing my praises."

"It's the least I could do," she said. "Considering you've been so attentive."

Was she teasing him? Flirting with him? Her eyes were sparkling as she tossed her glossy hair over her shoulder. Suddenly, he wished he'd had more personal protection training, although he suspected this wasn't in the rule book. The men he'd guarded before had been dignitaries or businessmen, not gorgeous, young—What was the word again?—Influencers.

"How about another beer? You're off duty now." Technically, yes, but she was still his responsibility. While he was on this assignment, he would never be fully off-duty.

"Sure." He wouldn't drink it all—just a few sips to be sociable. He felt they were building a rapport now, which was good. It made things less awkward. It would do her good to get used to him being around, to start trusting him, even if he found her presence... complicated. But that was his problem, not hers.

He got two beers out of the mini-fridge and handed her one.

"Here's to a productive week." She lifted the bottle, her eyes meeting his.

He ignored the flutter in his belly, clinked it, and took a long pull.

"What's your story, Viper?" She leaned back in her chair and studied him. "I know you are ex-military and Pat speaks highly of you, but apart from that, I don't know anything about you."

He shrugged. Where to start? What did you tell your principle about your personal circumstances? Usually very little. Keep it professional.

"Are you married?" That definitely wasn't in the rule book.

"No," he replied, a little too quickly.

"Significant other?" She raised an eyebrow.

"There's no one."

She smiled, like she was pleased to hear it. They were verging into dangerous territory here. Talking about his personal life was not his strong suit.

"And why is that? A guy like you must have plenty of options." She raked him over with her gaze.

He hesitated, then took a seat opposite her. "I'm not in the right frame of mind for a relationship."

She tilted her head to the side. "Oh, why's that?"

"Do you always ask so many questions?"

She chuckled. "Actually, yes. I guess I do. I'm a curious person and you're… Well, you're interesting."

Interesting? Well, he guessed that was better than boring.

"Being in the military doesn't lend itself to long-term relationships. I'm away a lot, coming and going at short notice. It's not fair to put that on someone."

"But you're not in the Navy anymore," she pointed out.

He ground his jaw, refusing to let her see how much that statement bothered him. "No, I'm not."

He was still getting used to being out. It was a hell of an adjustment, one he hadn't been handling too well, until Blade had come along. He touched the scar on his temple, a permanent reminder of just how hard it was to adjust.

Her eyes softened. "Well, the Navy's loss is my gain."

"That's nice of you to say, ma'am."

"Don't you think you can call me Izzy now?"

He bit his lip. "I'm not sure. It doesn't sound right, ma'am. This job is important to me. I don't want to come across as unprofessional."

"Well, I wouldn't want you to feel uncomfortable."

She snapped her laptop shut and got to her feet. "I'm going to bed. Thanks for helping me with Hernández." She hesitated, like she was about to say something else, but then decided not to.

"You're welcome."

He watched as she disappeared through the connecting door to her suite and closed it behind her. He listened for the click, but it didn't come.

She hadn't locked it.

CHAPTER 11

"*D*on't look at me like that." Izzy pursed her lips in the perfect pout. "It's just a little yacht party."

They were in his suite at the hotel, and she'd just broken the news to him about this evening's outing. As expected, he was not happy about it.

"I thought we agreed you weren't going to take any more risks."

"This isn't a risk. Casper is an old friend of Robert's. They studied together at Yale. I've met him several times before. He's harmless."

Viper ran a hand through his hair, clearly agitated.

"You can check him out, he's squeaky clean. Actually, scratch that. He's an investment banker—they're never squeaky clean." She scoffed. "But he has no ties to my father's business. No interest in the mines."

"It's not that," Viper said tersely. "It's being out in the open. Anyone could take a shot at you in the marina. It's unprotected, there are lots of places to hide. I can't be everywhere at once."

"We'll be on a yacht, moored at the marina. Nobody is going to get to me on board."

He hesitated, but she could see she was getting to him.

"Come on, this'll be fun. I don't want to stay cooped up here the whole time."

His chiseled jaw ground together so hard she could see the muscles moving.

"It's not like a bar or a club, it's a private yacht. I'll know half the guests there and the other half will be friends of Casper's."

He sighed, and she knew she'd won him over.

"Robert was only supposed to come next week," he pointed out. "Why the sudden change of plan?"

She smiled at his grumpiness. "He's tied up all next week, so he came for a few days this week. Suits me better, actually, because it means I'll have next week to myself."

"Will he be staying with you?" Viper's expression was neutral, but his eyes zoomed in on her face.

She frowned. "No, of course not. We're not dating."

"I'm sorry to pry, but I've got to ask so I can adapt your security."

"That's okay, and no, Robert will have his own room."

Another curt nod, but she thought she saw a flash of relief cross his face. Or was that her wishing it was so? With him, she couldn't be sure. He was always so guarded.

Last night was about as personal as he'd ever gotten with her. She could understand why he hadn't had a relationship in the Navy, but now he was a free agent. Although, he hadn't been out long. Pat had said only a few months.

She'd read about how hard it was for servicemen to adjust to civilian life. Was he going through that now? He didn't give away a thing. If he was stressed, he wasn't showing it.

"We're meeting the others in the hotel bar at seven," she said.

"Yes, ma'am."

Izzy stared at the two dresses on her bed. The silver one was soft and slinky and demanded attention. She certainly wouldn't go unnoticed in that. The black one clung to her like an oil slick that changed color when she moved. It was sexy as hell but more "rock chick" than "cocktail hour glam".

"Viper," she called. She'd purposely left the connecting door between their two rooms open, and although he hadn't come through it at all, she'd heard him walking around, taking a shower, getting dressed. It was intimate, in a weird kind of way.

He immediately appeared in the doorway. "Yes?" Then froze when he saw her standing in a towel robe.

"I can't decide which dress to wear. What do you think?"

He didn't move. "You want me to choose?"

"Yes, I need a man's opinion."

He shook his head and came a bit closer. "The black one."

"Hmm... Interesting choice. Why did you pick that one?" Her mind whirred. Was it the rough-and-ready part of him? Did he like a wild child as opposed to a glamour puss? Maybe he was into rock music? He looked the type. That sexy-as-hell tattoo on his chest, right over his heart.

"It'll make you less of a target."

And he turned on his heel and left the room.

Great.

Izzy sighed and flopped on the bed. The man was impossible!

She didn't know why he made her so mad, but he did.

Maybe it was because she couldn't crack him. Every man she'd ever known had hit on her. Even the ones professing to be her friends. Everywhere she went she was fawned over, idolized. It was partly because of who she was and partly because of what she looked like.

A style icon, she'd been called in the media. A role model for millions of young women. She was also a success story, a businesswoman, an entrepreneur in her own right. And of course, her family legacy made her a wealthy debutante.

The exotic, sultry looks she'd inherited from her Brazilian mother meant she drew attention. Designers wanted her to wear their clothes. Magazines wanted her to grace their covers. She was always being given jewelry or outfits or the latest gadget to try out in hopes that she'd give it a stellar online review. Her Instagram account had over two million followers. Her opinion mattered. Her fans adored her. Men wanted to sleep with her.

Except *he* wasn't like that.

He kept his distance, even when he was standing right beside her. That cool, aquamarine gaze stared through her rather than at her, refusing to engage. He was driving her crazy.

With a huff, she pulled on the silver dress. It was slinky and sexy and had tiny spaghetti straps that crossed at the back. You couldn't wear a bra with it.

Around her neck hung the turquoise necklace.

Just before seven, Viper poked his head through the connecting door. "Are you ready, Miss Beaumont?"

"Yes."

His gaze flickered over her dress, but he didn't comment.

They went downstairs to the hotel bar. Him first, surveying the corridor, the elevator, and the lobby, before she stepped into it. He looked sexy as hell bursting out of that black suit, with a matching black shirt underneath exposing just a glimpse of his tanned chest, but she knew the Kevlar vest was beneath it, and that he was armed.

Women turned to stare.

She couldn't help but feel smug that this Adonis of a man was with her. In her slinky silver dress, they made quite a pair, and she almost took his arm like she would any of her other male admirers, only just stopping herself in time. Holy hell, that was close. She must get a hold of herself.

"There you are!" Emily rushed over. "Look who I found."

Izzy broke into a practiced smile. "Hello, Robert."

"Darling!" He embraced her, kissing her on both cheeks. "I hope you don't mind me turning up early. It was the only time I could get away."

Viper bristled beside her.

"No, of course not. It's lovely to see you."

"Who is this?" Robert eyed Viper, and not in a good way. Oh, he kept his cool—of course he would, it was Robert—but she didn't miss the flash of jealousy in his gaze.

"This is my bodyguard, Viper. Viper, this is Robert Hampton-Barnes, CEO of Omega Enterprises." She used Robert's full title to give his ego a boost. Standing next to the towering Viper, he needed all the help she could give him.

As expected, Robert puffed out his chest, although it still fell pathetically short of Viper's, who wasn't even trying. The differences didn't end there. While Robert was lithe and slender, cutting a fine figure in a tailored suit, Viper was broad and muscular, exuding a powerful energy that was hard to ignore. Robert was all dignified calm, while Viper simmered with a dangerous, but controlled aggression.

"Bodyguard? Surely you don't need him tonight. We'll be on Casper's yacht. Give him the night off."

"I'm afraid that's out of the question, sir," Viper said.

Robert put his arm around her. "She'll be fine, she's with me."

"It's okay, Robert," Izzy cut in. The two men were glaring at each other. "He can come."

Robert's mouth straightened into a thin line. "As you wish, darling."

Izzy wished he wouldn't call her darling, although it was almost worth it to see the way Viper's lips compressed into a thin line when he did. Was her personal protection officer jealous? Was she finally getting a reaction out of him?

Robert bought them a drink, while Viper stood a few feet away. She stood side-on to him, so she couldn't see his expression, but by the way Emily kept glancing nervously at him, she knew he was glaring daggers at her.

"What have you done to piss him off?" her friend whispered, when Robert moved away a little to greet someone else. "He looks like he's about to explode."

"He's not happy about this party," Izzy confided, although that was only half the truth. Robert had encroached on his territory by insisting she give him the night off. He hadn't liked that.

"Too bad," sang Emily. "It'll be fun. You could do with letting your hair down a bit. He'll just have to deal with it."

Robert came back and slipped an arm around her waist. She was used to it. Ever since her father had died, he'd treated her like a little girl who needed protection. Used to the attention, it had never occurred to her to mind, but when she turned around and saw Viper's blazing gaze, she swallowed and took a step back.

"What's wrong?" Robert asked her.

"Nothing." She forced a smile. "It's warm in here, isn't it?"

He shrugged and carried on talking.

When she glanced back at Viper, he was staring over her head at the wall behind her.

CHAPTER 12

$\mathcal{V}$iper was seething, but he fought hard not to show it. Adaptability was his middle name, but he preferred knowing the plans in advance. It made it easier to anticipate the risks.

They left the hotel and walked the short distance to the marina. Yachts of all shapes and sizes bobbed on the inky blue water, their white hulls shining in the moonlight. It was a perfect evening. Still, balmy, not a breath of air.

High Yield was a forty-five-foot luxury yacht with a silver hull and a smart mahogany deck. It was also lit up like a goddamn Christmas tree. A sniper would have no problem locating the guests through his scope. Fairy lights twinkled on the railings and a warm amber glow emanated from within. Music swept off the deck accompanied by the sound of laughter and tinkling champagne glasses.

"Wow," gasped Emily, who must have seen her fair share of yachts. "She's beautiful."

"Welcome aboard." Robert offered a hand to help the women onto the deck, then pulled himself up, positioning himself to block Viper's way.

Unfazed, Viper scanned the dock before springing aboard. Boats were second nature to him. Typically, he approached via wet insertion, scaling the sides with caving ladders and using climbing gear. The ease of this boarding wasn't lost on him.

On deck, he surveyed the yacht. She was a beauty, no doubt about that. The soft listing made him feel right at home. It took him less than a second to find his sea legs.

"God, I feel like I'm already drunk," laughed Emily, clutching Izzy's arm.

"You'll get used to it." Robert strode ahead past a covered jet ski. Viper didn't miss the arrogant swagger. This was his domain. These were his people. "Come on, let's find Casper."

Viper followed, analyzing the threat level. About fifty guests dressed in evening wear. The hot weather meant many had discarded their blazers. Shirts without jackets meant fewer places to hide weapons.

Threat level minimal, so far.

At least the yacht was a contained space, he could mitigate the risk onboard.

"Great, you're here!" sang a male voice. A rotund man in an unashamedly pink shirt came to welcome them. He had a cigar in one hand and a glass of champagne in the other. "Now we can set off."

"What?" burst out Viper.

Robert glowered. "Oh, that's Izzy's security detail. Got a stick up his ass."

Viper clenched his fists. He'd like to shove that stick up Robert's ass.

Izzy touched his arm. "Don't mind him. He's just jealous."

He frowned, unsure what she meant. Jealous of what? There was nothing going on between them. No reason to be jealous. It was obvious Robert had designs on Izzy, and she wasn't fighting him off.

The luxury yacht got underway. He felt the powerful engines kick in as it reversed out of its berth and then thrust forward into the midnight-blue bay. The smell of the sea swept him back to his training days when everything was fresh and exciting. Untold adventures lay ahead. Who would have thought that a decade later it would have all gone to shit?

Izzy and Emily got a drink and mingled among the other guests. He watched the heiress work her magic. It was effortless, a warm smile here, a touch of the arm there.

How is your sister? I haven't seen her in forever. No, the Hamptons were dreadful. Overrun by tourists, couldn't wait to leave. San Diego is so revitalizing.

Every now and then she'd glance at him, just to make sure he was still there.

The evening wore on. They finally anchored about twenty miles out to sea. San Diego was a sparkling jewel in the distance.

Viper did a lap of the yacht and returned to where Izzy was talking to Robert on the deck. He felt on edge but didn't know why. Arguably, they were safer here than back in the marina. Out here, there was nobody around to take a shot at her. Still, he knew better than most that just because you were out in the ocean, it didn't mean there were no threats.

Robert had steered Izzy away from the rest of the party. Viper approached silently but stood a respectful distance away. As much as he didn't like the self-entitled prick, it wasn't his place to judge. Izzy's life was her own, and he had no say in who she dated.

Robert, who'd been talking in earnest, glanced up and frowned. "For Pete's sake, can't we have a moment's privacy?"

Izzy tensed, he saw it in her shoulders. "It's his job, Robert."

"Well, there's nowhere to go here," he said with a snort. "Tell him to get lost."

"He can stay," she said tartly.

Viper barely concealed his grin.

Robert huffed but resumed their conversation in a hushed voice. Viper heard the words "iron ore" and "the company" as well as "members of the board." They were talking shop. He turned away.

A low hum caught his attention. It sounded like an outboard motor.

Alarm bells fired off in his brain. He stared out to sea, but it was pitch black and he had zero visibility. The flickering fairy lights on the railings didn't help.

"What's wrong?" asked Izzy, noticing his agitation. He liked that she was in tune with him. Robert didn't have her entirely captivated, just yet—but he couldn't focus on that now.

"I don't know. I thought I heard something."

"What? Out there?" She too gazed into the darkness off the bow.

"There's nothing out there but ocean," scoffed Robert, glancing around. "You're paranoid."

Viper listened hard, but the sound had vanished, yet the hairs on the back of his neck prickled. Over the years he'd learned to trust his gut. Slowly, he reached for his gun.

Two other couples had wandered out onto the bow, but most of the guests were at the stern, which was designed for entertaining and had easy access to the bar.

He peered over the side into the water.

Nothing.

The prickling moved to his arms. Something was definitely up.

A shot echoed through the night air, making everybody

jump. Seconds later, four armed men in ski masks leaped over the guard railing onto the deck.

Fuck!

He was on the wrong side.

Viper raced toward Izzy, firing at the attackers in order to create some kind of cover. They returned fire and he had no choice but to dive behind the leather seats. His Glock was no match for four semi-automatic weapons.

"Get down!" he yelled.

The guests screamed and ran back inside. All except Robert, who stood rooted to the spot. Izzy screamed as a black-clad man swooped her up and tossed her overboard into the waiting motorboat.

"Izzy, no!"

Viper belly-crawled out from behind the seat only to duck back again when a hail of bullets rained down on him. He was outgunned, and he fucking knew it. There was nothing he could do. He couldn't get to her without ripping himself to pieces.

Robert cried out as a bullet nicked his arm. The idiot was still standing up in full sight, staring at the kidnappers like a deer in headlights. He might not be able to get to Izzy, but he could reach Robert. Viper lurched forward, grabbed him, and pulled him back down behind the seats as another torrent of bullets flew overhead. If the idiot had still been upright, he'd be a dead man.

Something glittery caught his eye. He glanced down and saw it was Izzy's turquoise pendant. It must have come loose in the struggle.

The outboard motor sprang to life and the men jumped over the railing back onto the craft. As soon as they'd stopped firing, Viper took off across the deck.

"I'm shot. Help me. I've been shot," cried Robert, clutching his bleeding arm.

Viper gripped the railing and stared out after the inflatable. He watched as it disappeared into the darkness, its black hull a mere shadow in the glow of the superyacht. It was designed for stealth over speed. He gauged the outboard motor to be at least fifty horsepower.

Viper thought hard. It would take too long for the yacht to pull up anchor, and he didn't particularly want to lead fifty wealthy partygoers into a shootout with a bunch of pirates.

That left the jet ski.

He raced along the gangway to the stern and ripped the cover off the machine, before pushing it onto the launch pad. In the background, he could hear Robert still yelping on the deck.

"Call 911 and the Coast Guard," he shouted to Emily, who'd come out to see if the coast was clear.

"Is Izzy all right?" Her face was ashen.

"No, she's been taken, and Robert's been shot."

"Oh, God." Her hands flew to her mouth.

"Call, now!"

Emily was still fumbling for her phone as he pushed the jet ski out, leaped on, and took off after the retreating motorboat.

CHAPTER 13

*V*iper raced after the kidnappers, pushing the jet ski to its maximum capacity. He didn't hold out much hope, but he had to try.

They'd be taking her to a mothership, by the looks of things. They were too far away from the shore for the inflatable to make it back and their current bearing was south. There must be a bigger craft out there somewhere.

He kept the shadowy vessel in his sights as he floored the tiny engine. It didn't hold much gas, and soon the gauge was flickering above empty. Looking up, he couldn't see the boat. Panic threatened to surge through his veins, but he focused on remaining calm. He knew it was the only way through this. Lose it, and he'd lose Izzy.

"Come on," he muttered, scanning the dark surface of the ocean. "Where are you?"

There!

In the distance, he spotted a murky, dark hull rising out of the water. It was swathed in darkness, all the lights off on deck, but he could make out a white bulkhead. It looked to be a commercial vessel of some kind. A fishing trawler maybe?

He grunted. Good cover. No one would look twice at a fishing boat docking in the early hours.

The jet ski's engine spluttered, then hiccupped as it jerked spasmodically. He'd never make it back to the yacht, but then he'd known that right from the start. No point in holding back, so he pushed every last inch out of the machine before it stalled.

The night was eerily silent, save for the gentle lapping of water against the jet ski. From here, he couldn't hear the inflatable anymore, but he could make out the name on the side of the ship: *Pacific Pride*.

The stealthy inflatable vanished around the darker hull of the ship, and he waited, picturing them docking and forcing Izzy on board. He was just debating whether or not he could swim out to it when he heard the engines churn.

Shit, they were leaving.

With a sinking heart, he watched the white foam churn at the stern as the vessel made a lazy turn and headed south, away from San Diego. It could be going anywhere, but his guess was Mexico.

He slammed his hands down on the handlebars. Damn it. He'd lost her.

The only thing he had was a name.

Pacific Pride.

It wasn't much, but it was better than nothing.

The Coast Guard picked him up a couple of hours later. The jet ski had a light at the front, like a motorcycle, which he'd kept on. Luckily, they'd located him before the battery had died.

He took the GPS coordinates from the captain, knowing full well that he would have drifted over the course of the last few hours, and he gave them the name of the fishing vessel.

They looked it up on their sonar, but it was nowhere to be seen.

The fishing trawler had vanished.

As soon as Viper stepped back on dry land, he called Blackthorn Security HQ in D.C. and told Blade what had happened.

There was no blame, no reprimand for losing his principal, just a terse exchange of the facts. Viper told Blade what he knew, gave him the coordinates and the name of the ship, and the Operations Manager instructed him to sit tight. They'd get back to him.

Viper paced up and down his hotel room. What an almighty fuckup. How could this have happened? Nobody had known they were going out on that yacht tonight. It had been a last-minute decision, and yet, that attack had been planned and executed to perfection. A quick, violent ambush. They'd grabbed the target and gotten out of there, all in under five minutes.

Those guys were pros. The semi-automatics they'd been using were proof of that. AK-47 assault rifles. He'd recognized the distinctive curved magazines from his time in the Middle East.

The telephone rang. It was the hotel reception asking him to come downstairs. A detective from the San Diego Police Department had arrived to interview him.

"Have you found the trawler?" he asked, as soon as the introductions were out of the way.

"Not yet." The stocky, mustached detective gestured for him to sit down. "I'd like to hear your version of the events?"

Viper sighed but eased himself into a chair in the reception waiting area. This was a waste of time. He got that the police had to do their thing, but without a trace on the ship, they wouldn't get anywhere. He gave an impatient summary of what happened and then said he had to go. There was one person he was dying to see.

Robert.

That man was the only one who'd known about the party in advance. It had been his idea to go. His friend who'd hosted it. Viper wanted some answers.

He took a cab to the hospital where Robert was being treated. A flesh wound, the doctor said. They'd stitched him up and given him some antibiotics and painkillers. He should be able to go home soon.

"What do you want?" Robert barked as Viper marched into the room.

A thank you would be nice, Viper thought. He'd only saved the jerk's ass, but instead he said, "We need to talk."

Robert looked wary. "It was your job to protect her. You failed. What is there to talk about?"

Okay, he was pushing it. Viper took a steadying breath. Luckily he'd been trained to withstand assholes. Besides, he had more important things to do than argue with Robert. Izzy's life was at stake. "You wanted me to stay behind, remember?"

Robert frowned. "You don't think I had anything to do with this?"

Viper gave him a penetrating look. "That's what I'm trying to find out. You didn't want me onboard. You made that very clear. Why was that?"

Robert stared at him for a long moment, then sighed. "Okay, if you must know, I wanted to get Izzy alone. I needed to talk to her about something."

"About what?"

"None of your business."

"In light of what's happened, it is my business. If you don't want to be a suspect in her abduction, then you better start talking."

Robert leaned back on the pillow. "Okay, relax. Izzy and I have been seeing quite a lot of each other over the last few months, and I wanted to talk to her about our relationship."

Viper scowled.

"I wanted to take it to the next level. I was going to tell her how I felt about her, and I didn't want a big oaf like you hanging around when I did it."

Viper studied him. He seemed legit. There was even a faint blush in the middle of his cheeks that hinted of wounded male pride.

We're not together.

Had Izzy lied about their relationship? Was there something between them?

Nah, there couldn't be. He recalled the way she'd been dancing with those men at the club. There was no way she was committed to this guy.

She didn't want to rip his clothes off. Wasn't that what she'd said to Emily?

It seemed Robert's feelings were not returned. Unrequited love. It was a bitch.

"Who else knew about the party on the yacht?" he asked.

"Nobody. It was a last-minute thing. I wasn't even supposed to be here until next week. After I changed my plans, I rang Casper to tell him I'd be in town, and he invited us to the party. Naturally, I asked Izzy to join me."

"Who is Casper? Do you know him well?"

"Yeah, we studied together at Yale. I can vouch for him. He's a stellar guy."

I'm sure.

Viper thought for a moment. Casper had no reason to kidnap Izzy, nor did he have anything against her father, that they knew of. He could be in it with Robert, but Izzy had said herself, Robert couldn't afford to buy her out. She was more useful to him alive than dead. He had no motive.

Still, he'd given Blade both their names. They would do a more thorough check, including a search for outstanding warrants, previous records, or any other criminal activity. At the moment, however, it looked like this dickhead was in the clear.

"Did you tell anyone else about the party?"

"No, I wasn't even sure I was going until I'd spoken to Izzy. If she didn't want to, I wouldn't have gone."

Viper very much doubted that. Robert wasn't the type of guy to sacrifice his evening for someone else, even a woman he professed to be in love with.

"How's the shoulder?" he asked.

"Freaking painful."

Good, thought Viper, as he left the room. Served him right for taking Izzy onto the yacht and putting her in harm's way. And for being a prick.

His next stop was Emily.

Izzy's personal assistant opened the door, her face wet with tears. To her credit, she looked awful. Her eye makeup was smudged and running down her cheeks, she still wore her wrinkled party dress from last night, and it was clear she hadn't slept a wink.

"Any news?" She wiped her eyes with the back of her hands.

"I'm afraid not."

Marching back into the room, she threw herself onto the bed. "Poor Izzy! God only knows what those monsters are doing to her now."

Viper preferred not to think about that, but he did know that if it was the cartel and they planned to ransom her or use her as a bargaining chip, it was in their best interests to keep her alive. This wasn't piracy in the traditional sense, although he did have some experience of that. One year, while deployed on a warship off the coast of East Africa, he'd had several run-ins with well-funded, organized crime groups operating from motherships with the sole purpose of stealing crude oil from tankers. They used excessive force and didn't bother with kidnapping for ransom. Any hostages or casualties were shot and killed. It was easier that way.

The men who'd taken Izzy were not interested in oil. They had something else in mind, something to do with her father's company.

"I'm sure she's fine," he said with more confidence than he felt. "They won't hurt her. She's too valuable as leverage."

"Do you think so?" she sniffed.

He nodded. "Emily, I need to ask you a question. Did you know about the party on the yacht before Robert arrived?"

She thought for a moment. "Yes, I know Casper from the social scene in D.C. and he texted me an invite days ago, but I hadn't replied. It was up to Izzy."

Everything was up to Izzy, it seemed.

Everybody danced to her tune.

"Did the two of you discuss it?" he asked.

"We might have done," she admitted, sitting up. "Yes, we did. Casper came around to the hotel yesterday morning. We had drinks and he asked us again. Izzy said we'd play it by ear, depending on the shooting schedule."

"Did you discuss it with anyone else?

"I don't think so. Oh, wait a minute, the golfers were there."

"Golfers? You mean those men you were talking to at the pool?" He'd noticed them but deemed them not a threat. Maybe he'd been too hasty.

"Yes." She flushed. "I met up again with them that night you and Izzy left the club."

He narrowed his eyes. "Are they staying here?"

She flushed. "Matt is in room 375."

"Thanks, Emily." It was time to pay them a visit.

Room 375 was situated on the third floor of the hotel, two below theirs. Viper knocked on the door and waited.

There was no answer. After knocking a second time, he went back down to reception.

"Could you tell me if the guys in room 375 are still here? One of them left his shirt on the golf course yesterday. I thought I'd return it."

She looked at her computer screen.

"No, sir. I'm afraid they've already checked out."

Interesting.

"Any idea when?"

"Last night." She frowned. "But it says here they're paid up until today."

Now that was very interesting.

BLADE WILSON RANG him a couple of hours later. It was almost midday, and Viper still hadn't slept. His body wouldn't shut down. Not while Izzy was still out there. It had been fourteen hours since she'd been taken.

The police had been in touch. They'd immediately launched a kidnapping investigation, but with nothing concrete to go on, there wasn't much they could do. They'd put out an alert for the fishing trawler, *Pacific Pride,* but those guys were professionals—the boat would be long gone by now.

"What have you got?" he asked Blade as soon as he answered the phone.

"Nothing yet. One of our operatives, Phoenix, is on his way to you. He boarded a plane an hour ago. He'll make his way to the hotel. You'll need some help getting her back."

Adrenaline shot through his body. The mission wasn't over.

"I know Phoenix," he said. "We went through SEAL training together."

"Yeah, he's a great guy. I'm sorry we can't spare any more

operatives. As you know, we're under-resourced right now. Pat even suggested I come out, but I'm needed here."

"Did you find the fishing trawler?" Viper asked.

"Not yet. It's registered out of El Salvador, but that's not unusual."

His heart sank. Without a bead on the trawler, they had no hope of finding her.

"There is someone who we think can locate it," Blade added.

"Really? Who?"

"Phoenix's wife, Ellie, has a geologist friend at Stanford University who has access to a satellite. He maps the ocean floors along the coastline, mostly in the Gulf of Mexico. Something to do with finding oil deposits. There's a chance he has access to the live data from last night."

"Phoenix is married?" That was news. The Phoenix he'd known back in his SEAL days was the last person Viper would have guessed would settle down.

"Yeah, he met his wife on an oil rig in the Gulf last year. She's smart, like Lily. Don't know what these clever women want with us thugs."

Lily, Blade's wife, was a military software designer who worked for the US government. Anna had told him all about it when he'd been at the office.

"This friend of Ellie's, he'll help us track the *Pacific Pride*?"

"He should be able to. I'm sending you his contact details. Ellie has already spoken to him, so he's expecting your call."

"I'll get straight on it. Thanks, man."

"We'll get her back, brother. Don't worry."

He just hoped they'd get there in time.

CHAPTER 15

$\mathcal{R}$ay, the Stanford geologist, was eager to help.

"Sure, I can tap into the satellite for you. Those coordinates you supplied will help. Give me an hour and I'll call you back. Can I reach you on this number?"

"Yep. Thanks."

Viper went back to the hotel room to try to get some shut-eye, but everything reminded him of Izzy. Not even sure why, he walked into her room. There was that black dress lying on the bed. The room smelled of her perfume. He could almost see her parading around in front of him.

Fuck. How could he let this happen?

Going back to his room, he lay down on the bed and forced his exhausted brain to think. Who were the golfers? Were they the kidnappers? There'd been four of them. Four masked men on the yacht. They hadn't looked Mexican, although that didn't necessarily mean they weren't affiliated with the cartels. If they were a hit squad, they might be freelance.

He must have fallen asleep because he woke up to a

hammering on the door. It felt like mere seconds had passed. A voice called out, "Viper, it's Phoenix."

He sprung up and opened the door. "Sorry. Didn't get much sleep last night."

They shook hands. Phoenix thumped him on the shoulder. "Good to see you again, buddy. It's been a while."

Viper stood back to let him into the room. "Yeah, last time I saw you we were heading down that mountain peak in Colorado in the pitch dark, struggling against a fifty-mile-per-hour gale-force wind with icy rain pelting us."

Phoenix laughed. "I heard you made it through."

"Piece of cake," retorted Viper, which made Phoenix laugh all the louder.

Phoenix hadn't changed. He was still ridiculously good-looking, fit, and well-dressed. Not a rough-around-the-edges bruiser like himself.

"I heard you got married," Viper said, as Phoenix dumped his backpack on the floor. "Congrats."

"Thanks, I still can't believe she said yes." His eyes crinkled. "And now you're working for Blackthorn Security. Small world."

"Yep."

Phoenix studied him. "Pat is pretty picky. But then I heard you did good things out in Colombia a few months back."

Viper grimaced. His shoulder still ached, even though he'd completely healed up. The wounds in his side and thigh didn't bother him as much. He didn't like to talk about Colombia. He hadn't done anything monumental. Sure, he'd helped a few civilians escape when an out-of-town resort had been overrun with guerrillas, but any member of his unit would have done the same thing. It was what they were trained to do, after all. He'd just been in the right place at the wrong time.

"It might be the shortest-lived assignment in history."

"Nah, we'll get her back. Bad luck what happened, though. Wasn't your fault."

Viper ground his jaw. "I shouldn't have let her go anywhere near that goddamned yacht. I had a bad feeling about it right from the get-go."

"Why don't you get me up to speed?" Phoenix sat down at the table. "Then we can decide on a plan of action."

Viper briefed him about the party aboard the yacht, mentioning Robert and Casper, as well as Emily and her four golfing buddies.

"You think it could be them?" Phoenix asked, getting straight to the point.

"Maybe. Emily admitted she told them about the party. Four of them. Four kidnappers—all armed with AKs, Kevlar vests, the works. These guys were pros."

"Mercs?" Phoenix asked.

Viper nodded. "Without a doubt."

Phoenix nodded. "How'd you get on with Ray, the geologist?"

"I'm expecting a call anytime now," he said, checking his phone. There were no missed calls. "Also, I've asked hotel housekeeping not to clean the golfers' rooms, just in case the cops want to send forensics up there."

"Good thinking," said Phoenix. "The FBI is sending a team to take over the investigation. They'll definitely want to hear about the golfers."

Pat had been busy.

The phone rang. Viper dived for it. "Hello, Ray?"

"Good news," the geologist said. "I've found your ship."

Viper caught his breath.

Thank God.

He put him on speakerphone. "Go ahead."

"Well, thanks to your coordinates, I picked her up twenty-five miles off the coast of San Diego. She traveled directly south to Guadalupe Island, and then continued further down to the Revillagigedo Islands. Currently, she's roughly a hundred and fifty miles off the coast of Baja California."

"Mexico?" blurted Phoenix.

"Hey, is that you, Phoenix? I didn't know you were there too."

"Yeah, man. Got shipped in to get the girl back. You know how it is."

Viper didn't know they knew each other.

Ray chuckled. "No rest for the wicked. Anyway, I hope that helps."

"It sure does," said Viper. "Let us know if anything changes."

"Will do, although she hasn't shifted from that position for the last four hours."

"Thanks, man," echoed Phoenix.

They ended the call and looked at each other.

"How's your high-seas rescue game?" Phoenix asked.

Viper grinned. "Like riding a bike."

"It's madness without backup," said Blade on the phone from D.C., after Phoenix had told him what they planned to do.

"There's no time to get an amphibious task force out there," Phoenix argued. "It'll be hard enough with just the two of us."

"That's what I'm afraid of," replied Blade. "We haven't got resources in that part of the world. You know what it's like out there. Finding a chopper will be almost impossible."

"We're infiltrating by boat," said Phoenix. There wasn't any time to network and build up local contacts, so they'd have to just steal one if they couldn't hire one.

Viper listened to the conversation from across the room. He'd already packed his rucksack.

"I'll have a CIA jet waiting for you at the airport," said Blade. "They'll fly you out to Baja and supply you with weapons and kit, but apart from that, my hands are tied. I can't sanction a CIA-assisted rescue. Their boys aren't trained for this, and we don't know how many we're dealing with. You're going in blind. No intel."

"It's not a container ship," cut in Viper. "It's a fishing trawler. There were four guys who attacked us and they'll probably have one or two more on board. Worst case scenario, we're looking at six tangos." It was remarkable how easily he'd slipped back into the SEAL lingo.

"Six to two, that's a big ask, especially without support."

"Nothing we haven't faced before," said Phoenix grimly.

"Besides, they won't be expecting us," Viper cut in. The element of surprise gave them an advantage.

There was a pause.

"All right, guys. I can see you're set on this. Good luck. Bring her home."

"Roger that," they chorused.

CHAPTER 16

*I*zzy was terrified. She'd been in this squalid, stinking cabin all night and now the sun was up—she could see it shining through the grubby porthole—she still had no idea who had kidnapped her or why.

Of course, it must have something to do with the mine in Mexico and her father's death. A psycho stalker or obsessed fan wouldn't hire a small army to abduct her off a yacht. She had yet to put faces to her attackers.

The fishing trawler had bucked and rolled as they sailed through the night. At first, she'd felt so ill, she'd puked in the bucket in the corner of the room, but after a couple of hours, it had subsided. Although drained, she wasn't nauseous anymore, thank God.

Now the ship seemed to have stopped moving, if you could call it that. It still bopped and weaved, listing one way and then the other, but the engines were silent. At one point, she thought she'd heard the anchor roll down.

The thick porthole window was her only light source and she spent most of her time staring out of it, but all she could see was the dark green ocean stretching for miles until it merged with the horizon.

The sky was as blue as it was in San Diego, so she guessed they were still off the California coast somewhere, although she had no idea where. They'd taken her phone as soon as they'd thrown her into the motorboat and tossed it overboard. Right now, it was lying at the bottom of the ocean.

Not that it did her any good there.

Her slinky silver dress and high-heeled sandals looked ridiculous out here, but they hadn't given her a change of clothes and she wasn't about to walk barefoot around this cabin. Judging by the grime on the floor, it hadn't been cleaned in decades.

The whole place reeked of fish. She'd smelled it as soon as she came on board. It was a sizable fishing trawler, three or four times the length of Casper's yacht, but it was weathered and run-down. A real rust-bucket.

Her stomach rumbled. She was hungry, but more than that, she was dying for a drink of water. Would they bother to feed her and give her water? Or were they planning on killing her eventually, in which case anything they gave her was a waste.

She stifled a sob. If she cried now, she'd never stop.

Her last vision was of Viper firing his gun at the attackers while he tackled Robert, getting him out of the firing line. Her bodyguard, her protector. Well, he hadn't managed to save her this time.

The door rattled, and she scuttled to the back of the room, crouching in the corner.

Oh, God. This is it. They've come to kill me.

It opened, and a man in a ski mask stood there. "Here's some food and water." He didn't come in, just put it on the floor inside the door and closed it again.

Once she was sure he'd gone, she fell on the water jug and

drank half of it in one go. She knew she ought to sip it, but she was so thirsty she couldn't control herself. The food was only a chunk of stale bread, but it tasted like a gourmet meal. She wolfed it down, for once grateful for the carbs. They would keep her strength up.

They obviously didn't want to get rid of her just yet. What did that mean? She doubted they'd want to talk her out of selling the mine when it was easier to kill her. No one would find her body if they tossed her overboard.

She went back to the window. The sea looked cold and uninviting. Was that to be her watery grave? A few dark clouds had gathered on the horizon and appeared to be rolling toward them. It looked like there was a storm coming.

In order to keep from panicking, she thought about the events leading up to her kidnapping. How had the assailants known she'd be on that yacht? She hadn't even known until that very afternoon.

Viper had been right all along. The party on the yacht had provided the perfect opportunity for a surprise attack. Isolated, miles away from land, with no protection other than one man with a handgun. Useless against four terrifying machine guns.

Viper.

She thought longingly of the man that had not left her side these last few days. What was he doing now? Would he get into trouble for losing her?

Pat would certainly have something to say about that. Viper would probably lose his job. Even now, he could be back in the States licking his wounds. She was a failed mission. An op that had gone wrong.

She stifled another sob.

Why did thinking about him make her so emotional? Or

was it the realization that no one was coming for her, that she was completely alone out here?

Nobody knew where she was.

Her only hope was that the kidnappers would negotiate with her. Her life for the mine. But when an organization resorted to kidnapping, they were usually past the point of negotiation.

Her dear father. He'd been so passionate about the project in Mexico.

"We've brought running water and electricity to the most inaccessible local communities," he'd told her proudly only last year.

Selfishly, she knew she'd give up the mine if it meant sparing her life. If it wasn't too late.

If only she'd taken her security more seriously. If only she'd listened to Viper. He'd tried to dissuade her, but she'd kept on until she'd gotten her way. Even Robert had tossed his concern aside, overridden it. And she'd done nothing to stop it.

This was her fault as much as his.

She felt the tears well up again. Not only would Viper lose his job, but he'd have her death on his hands, as well. She did cry after that. The tears spilled forth and she couldn't stop them.

Izzy curled up on the low bunk and hugged her knees, wishing she were anywhere but here.

CHAPTER 17

The sea was rougher than around San Diego. Out here in the Pacific, off the coast of Baja California, it got pretty wild. Huge, angry gray swells pummeled the coastline, and the rigid inflatable boat powered by a hundred horsepower engine soared over the peaks and troughs like a rollercoaster.

The motion would have sent them flying if they hadn't been used to it. Both men had their hands firmly wrapped around the guard rope, their grips unwavering. Their feet were anchored on the deck with the precision of seasoned navy men. As they leaned forward into the wind, their bodies moved instinctively, absorbing the bucketing and pounding with bent knees, honed from years of experience. The spray from the waves hit their faces, but their steely gazes remained fixed on the horizon, undeterred by the storm's fury.

Most of his offshore training had taken place in the Atlantic, but he was well used to these conditions, although Viper had to admit, it had been a while since he'd attempted a boarding operation. His last few missions had been in the Middle East, not on the ocean.

"How much longer?" he yelled at Phoenix, who was driving.

"ETA twelve minutes."

That's if Pacific Pride was where she was supposed to be. Their last update from Ray had put her at the same coordinates as before, so it looked like she'd put down anchor. They could only hope.

"Looks like that storm's coming in," Phoenix shouted above the wind and the roar of the engine. "Could make things tricky."

"Weather app said we had another five hours before landfall." Viper had checked before they'd left. They'd been trained to leave nothing to chance.

Still, they'd done these ship-boarding exercises a hundred times in all conditions. Tricky did not mean impossible.

"There she is," shouted Viper, who'd been spotting with a pair of high-powered binoculars. The CIA guys had been generous, even lending them a high-powered inflatable that was due to be transferred to Panama for use on the canal.

"Bring it back in one piece," the CIA Captain had said.

"We'll try," Viper had replied, although they both knew the likelihood of that happening was next to impossible.

They decreased speed and snuck up to the trawler. The black hull loomed above them, over a storey high. Phoenix kept the inflatable from bashing against the side of the trawler, but it was hard work and required constant adjustment on the tiller.

Viper attached the caving ladder to the telescopic pole. They were on the leeward side of the ship, tucked in beneath the hull and out of sight of anyone on deck.

"Easy," warned Phoenix.

Viper grimaced with determination. With a practiced

motion, he hooked the ladder over the guardrail. "Got it!" He collapsed the telescopic pole and set it back in the RIB, then put a gloved hand on the ladder. "See you soon."

"I'll be here," Phoenix confirmed.

Under normal circumstances there'd be at least four armed SEALs climbing onboard the ship and one manning the inflatable. They'd also have air support. Viper would have liked Phoenix to come aboard as backup, but he had to stay put.

"See you in a bit."

Rung by rung, he climbed up the ladder, keeping a steady motion and trying not to graze his hands on the hull when it listed. At the top, he glanced back down but couldn't see Phoenix thanks to his dark, camouflaged clothing.

Combat knife in hand, he stuck to the shadows as he slunk along the gangway, his back against the superstructure. Voices came from inside, men laughing and talking. He peered through a dirty, water-lashed window and counted five tangos. How many more were there?

He found the low door leading down to the interior of the trawler and descended, one careful step at a time, his knife in his hand. His handgun wasn't fitted with a suppressor, so if he encountered any opposition, he'd have no choice but to go loud.

That would bring the others running, and then it was over.

The trawler wasn't very big, only one room off the main cabin, and it was bolted from the outside.

Bingo.

He knocked on the door. "Izzy, are you in there?"

He heard scampering inside and a scared voice said, "Viper? Is that you?"

"Yes. I'm going to get you out."

"Oh, thank God."

He pulled the bolt back and opened the door.

She flew across the room and into his arms. "Oh, Viper. How did you find me? I'm so glad you're here. I thought they were going to kill me."

"Shh..." He gave her a quick hug, then released her. "Are you okay?"

She seemed to be in one piece. There was a nasty bruise on her upper arm where they'd manhandled her, but otherwise, she seemed fine.

"I'm okay."

He glanced at her shoes. "Ditch the heels. You can't run in those, and they'll make noise on the deck."

She looked at the dirty floor, then clenched her teeth and pulled off her shoes.

He took her hand. "Come on, we have to get out of here."

They snuck up the stairs onto the deck. The men were still joking around inside the bulkhead where it was warm and dry. Judging by the smell downstairs, they only went down there to sleep.

"Stay close," he told her, holstering his knife and racking the slide back on his gun. To hell with stealth now that he had her. If they had to go loud, so be it.

They snuck along the gangway, Izzy gripping his hand. It felt cold and small in his. They were almost at the point where the ladder hung when a shout echoed behind them.

Fuck. They'd almost made it out.

He turned and opened fire, pushing Izzy to the ground behind him. The man on patrol ducked behind the bulkhead, yelling for his buddies.

Glancing quickly over the side, he saw Phoenix's pale face staring upward through the darkness. They only had a few seconds before the others would descend on them, guns blazing. No time to climb down.

"Can you jump?" he yelled at Izzy. It was roughly ten feet high. Not impossible.

Face ashen, she nodded. "I think so."

"Go!"

Phoenix would know they had no choice and even now, he could hear the inflatable's motor kicking up foam, moving away from the hull.

Izzy climbed over the railing and hesitated. Viper did his best to keep firing at the kidnappers, forcing them to stay under cover. As soon as he stopped, they'd advance. He counted four, but that didn't mean there weren't others. They weren't wearing masks now, so he managed a brief but hard look at two of them.

"Now, Izzy!" he shouted over his shoulder.

She took a deep breath and launched herself off the deck. He watched her fall and hit the water, vanishing under the dark surface. At least he knew she could swim, although the unpredictable ocean was completely different from a hotel swimming pool.

A deluge of bullets pockmarked the deck in front of him.

That was it. Time to go.

He ran at the rail and dove over it, still holding his weapon. He turned in the air and hit the water butt-first, breaking his fall. Shots rained down over the side of the trawler. He swam toward the inflatable, praying none of them would find a mark.

Phoenix was hauling a shivering Izzy on board.

"Go!" he yelled, gripping the guard rope.

Phoenix didn't hesitate. As soon as Izzy was inside the boat, he twisted the throttle and the inflatable surged forward. Viper hung on for dear life until they were out of firing range, after which Phoenix slowed down and pulled him on board.

"That was a close one," Phoenix shouted into the wind.

The surface of the sea had been whipped into crests of whitewater. The storm was moving in fast.

"It's not over yet," warned Viper, glancing back at the ship. The kidnappers had launched their own motorboat and were getting ready to pursue. "Let's move."

Phoenix hit the throttle again and the bow rose into the air before flattening out as they raced over the bumpy surface.

Izzy sat in her tiny silver dress, eyes wide, teeth chattering uncontrollably, hanging on to the rope around the edge of the inflatable.

"You're safe now," Viper said.

Then, their pursuers opened fire.

CHAPTER 18

*I*zzy clenched her jaw and hung onto the rope for dear life. It felt like her teeth were rattling around in her head and the vibrations from the boat jingled every part of her body.

The kidnappers were still firing, but their shots sounded progressively farther away.

"We can outrun them," shouted Viper, grinning at his buddy, who she vaguely recognized from Pat's office.

What was he so happy about? They'd barely gotten away with their lives. And she'd never done anything as scary as jump off a ship before. Those men on the deck could have killed them.

She could still picture Viper diving off the side of the trawler, twisting in midair like some superhero action figure.

Even then he'd been smiling.

Freaking adrenaline junkies, the pair of them.

"I'll head straight for the coast." Phoenix focused ahead of the boat. "The most important thing is to find cover."

Viper fished under the seat for a warm sweater and

handed it to her. "Take this. You're shivering." He didn't seem to mind being in wet clothes.

She pulled it over her dress. It reached to her knees, but at least it was warm and dry. "Th—Thanks."

The motorboat behind them was getting smaller and smaller. Perhaps everything would be okay. As the adrenaline wore off, she began to tremble.

Viper sat beside her, careful to keep one hand on the guard rope at all times. She could tell he was an expert, the way he moved effortlessly around the inflatable, knees elastic, weight forward. Unlike her, still jiggling all over the place.

"Come here." He put his arm around her and she sank into his heat. How could his body temperature be so warm when he'd just come out of the freezing ocean? She was like a popsicle.

She snuggled into his side and put her head on his shoulder. His top was wet, but she didn't care. She needed to feel him, to touch him.

"I was so scared," she murmured. "I thought they were going to kill me."

"I know. It's okay now. We've got you."

Tears threatened, but she held them back. She couldn't cry now that it was over. Not in front of them.

"Thank you," she gasped as the wind whipped the words from her mouth. He felt so strong and capable, so reassuring. She nestled closer.

"No problem." He winked at her. "Just doing my job."

Slowly her shivers subsided.

They flew across the dark water toward the coast. At first, it was an ominous shadow up ahead, but then, as they got closer, it changed to a forest-green blur and the landmass began to take shape.

Trees covered the coastline like an impenetrable green wall, while waves crashed on the sandy shore, their white crests luminous in the moonlight.

"They're not giving up," muttered Viper, who was keeping a lookout.

Phoenix grimaced. "She's worth a lot of money."

"You think they were going to ransom me?" Izzy asked.

"It's one option," Phoenix said, vaguely.

"We think they were going to ransom you for the mine," Viper added.

"Oh, God," Izzy murmured through chattering teeth. "My life in exchange for the mining rights. The board would have no choice but to agree."

Viper glanced behind them. "Either way, they're not giving up. We're going to have to take cover in the jungle."

"The jungle?" She'd been so looking forward to a hot shower.

"That's all there is around here." Viper pointed toward the shore.

Izzy yelped and clung to the guard rope as they ramped over a giant wave and landed with a jolt. The inflatable rode the wave into shore until sand scraped the bottom of the boat.

"Let's go." Viper grabbed a small pack from the under-seat compartment and handed it to Izzy. "There are some dry clothes and shoes in there. When we get undercover, you can change."

"Oh, thank God." She couldn't picture herself running barefoot through the jungle in a cocktail dress.

Phoenix pulled out two more packs from the dry compartment beneath his seat and handed one to Viper. They leaped out of the boat.

Izzy clambered out far less elegantly, her bare feet sinking into the wet sand. The men hauled the boat up the beach to the cover of the trees and disguised it as best they could with branches and leaves. When they were done, it looked like just another tangled mesh of jungle foliage.

Izzy felt raindrops on her face and glanced upwards. "Could this day get any worse?"

Viper gestured up ahead. "Let's get under cover."

She gawked at the impenetrable green wall. "We're going in there?"

"Yep. Now would be a good time to put those shoes on."

She opened the backpack and pulled on a pair of sneakers. "You got these out of my closet?"

Viper nodded. "Thought you might need them."

She was amazed at his thoroughness, and the certainty that he'd find her. Hang on. How had they found her? She was about to ask when the hum of the approaching motorboat rose over the pitter-patter of the rain.

"Come on, we've got to move," Phoenix urged. Seconds later, they ducked into the sprawling vegetation. It instantly swallowed them up.

They surged forward, Viper in front with Phoenix right behind him. Izzy brought up the rear. She glanced nervously behind her, but the forest seemed to close around them, and she couldn't see the way back to the beach.

"How do you know we're not going round in circles?" she asked worriedly, a short while later. "Everything looks the same."

"Experience." Viper stared ahead into the darkness. "We've done a lot of jungle training over the years."

He must have fantastic night vision. She couldn't see more than two feet in front of her face. Phoenix moved effortlessly behind him, hardly making a sound in the undergrowth, while she was crashing about like a small elephant.

She could hear the rain above them, pelting down on the

jungle canopy, but it was so thick where they were that only a few drips managed to break through.

"They're bound to come looking," she choked out, feeling the grueling pace in her aching calves and exhausted thighs. She'd barely slept since her capture, just a few hours here and there, terrified they'd come for her during the night. Now, as she trudged inland, she could not keep her eyes open.

"A little further," urged Viper, stopping to look back. "Then you can rest."

She nodded, grateful that he'd been able to read her so easily.

He was still in his wet clothes which stuck to him like a second skin. He didn't seem bothered, though, rambling through the jungle like he was taking a Sunday stroll. Phoenix was the same, even whistling a soft tune to himself.

The further they went, the denser it got. Soon, she was slapping leaves and branches out of her face as she walked. Just when she was about to collapse, Viper called a halt.

"Let's take a break here," he said. "You can get changed and then we'll find someplace to shelter for the rest of the night."

Thank God.

"I'll keep watch." Phoenix disappeared back the way they'd come. She couldn't believe he was going to retrace their steps.

"He'll let us know when the kidnappers land," Viper told her. "But you're safe for now."

For now?

"How soon before we get to a hotel?"

He shrugged. "No idea. We didn't launch from this part of the mainland, so we'll have to see. There might not be anything around here for miles."

"Seriously?" Izzy felt like crying.

"Why don't you get out of that dress," he said, more gently. "Being warm and dry will make you feel better."

"Okay." She pulled off the sweater and looked in the pack. "You packed this?"

"Yeah. Sorry, I hope it's okay? I wasn't sure what to—"

"It's fine." He'd packed jeans and a T-shirt, as well as a pair of panties into the backpack. The thought of him rifling through her underwear, selecting what to bring, made her flush. It seemed so intimate.

He turned away.

She peeled off the dress and threw it onto the ground. She didn't want to ever see it again. Then, she pulled on the T-shirt and wriggled back into the warm sweater. Was it his, or just a spare he'd picked up somewhere?

She took off her shoes and put on the panties, followed by the jeans. At least her legs would be protected. They'd already been scratched by the foliage. With her socks and shoes back on, she felt almost normal again.

"Better?"

"Yes, thanks."

He picked up the silver dress. "We can't leave anything behind. Put this into your pack." She did as he said.

Viper handed her a bottle of water, which she eagerly chugged down. It beat the putrid jug of water they'd given her on the trawler.

"Better save some for later," he warned. "We don't know how long we're going to be out here."

She gazed up at him, blinking as a few errant raindrops hit her in the eye. "Where are we anyway?"

"Mexican coastline, I think."

"You think?"

He grinned. "We flew to Mexico City and caught a lift with the CIA to the coast, but I think we're somewhere south of Acapulco, judging by the terrain."

She had a vague idea of where Acapulco was, but she'd never been there. Her Mexican trips had only extended as far as the areas where her father had mines, and those were often rural and out of the way.

There was a soft rustling nearby and Viper immediately pulled her down into a crouch. "Stay still," he whispered.

She froze. Thank God for pilates, otherwise she'd never be able to hold this pose. The rustling grew louder.

Crap. That didn't sound human.

She jumped as something snorted behind her and gripped Viper's thigh. It was rock solid but she dug her fingertips in anyway, her heart hammering.

Another snort and some snuffling noises and a wild boar shuffled past, nose to the ground. Thankfully, it kept going, showing no interest in the humans hunkering down only a few meters away.

"Oh, God." She let go of his thigh and collapsed onto the ground. Not only did they have to worry about their pursuers, but also wild animals. The jungle was alive with the sounds of the night. Crickets chirping, a soft cooing sound that she couldn't place, and the occasional chatter of unfamiliar night animals.

"I'm really not an outdoorsy type of girl," she admitted, which made him chuckle.

"You're doing fine. Come on, let's move on."

Phoenix chose that moment to reappear, and she realized Viper had known exactly where he was, while she hadn't heard him approach at all.

"They've just landed," he informed them. "There are six of them. My guess is that they'll spread out and try to find us. They're all armed. AKs, by the looks of things."

Izzy felt weak.

They were here.

"Come on." Viper helped her to her feet. "Let's keep going."

Now that the threat was approaching from behind, they shifted positions. Phoenix waited for her to follow Viper and then brought up the rear. Both men had their weapons drawn.

Izzy suddenly felt very afraid.

CHAPTER 19

*V*iper pushed on, thankful he was wearing gloves. The branches were sharp and scratched at his hands. Behind him, he could hear Izzy's breath coming in short, sharp gasps. She was tiring. The rain didn't help. It wasn't heavy, but it was persistent, and every now and then they'd feel it seeping into their clothing or down their necks.

He couldn't blame her for being grumpy. She'd been through hell in the last twenty-four hours. They needed to find somewhere to rest without being spotted by the kidnappers who were no doubt gaining on them. They were pros and they didn't have Izzy slowing them down. There were more of them too, so they could spread out and cover more ground. It was only a matter of time before they were sighted.

He came to a ditch covered in vegetation. If they could burrow beneath the foliage, they might be able to hide Izzy. She couldn't go on much further. Even now, their pace had slowed considerably.

"Let's lay up here," he said to Phoenix, who was rotating in a hundred and eighty degrees behind them.

Phoenix turned to look and nodded. "It's as good a place as any."

Viper lifted some of the denser branches and burrowed in. Using his knife, he sliced away any sharp branches until the hollow was comfortable enough for Izzy to crawl into.

"You want me to lie in there?" she stared at him incredulously as he re-emerged. "What if there are bugs and spiders?"

"At least they aren't armed with AK-47s," Viper said dryly.

She bit her lip. "Are you coming with me?"

He glanced at Phoenix. "Nope, we're going to keep watch."

"But what if they find you?" There was a hint of panic in her voice.

"They won't, don't worry."

"We know how to take care of ourselves," Phoenix added, with an encouraging smile.

She glanced worriedly at them, then ducked her head and slithered into the burrow. "Just be careful," came her muffled response as they layered on even more vegetation.

"Don't come out, no matter what," Viper told her. "Wait until we come for you."

He thought he heard a muffled sob before he turned away. She'd be okay there for now. At least until they'd neutralized the threat.

It was time to deal with these guys.

"I'll go left," whispered Phoenix, pointing ahead.

Viper nodded and moved right. They'd fan out and eventually come into contact with the men following them, taking them out quietly. They didn't need to discuss it; they'd done this maneuver countless times on ops, though never on the same team.

It wasn't long before Viper spotted one of their pursuers. Dressed head to toe in black with a Kevlar vest, the guy moved expertly through the undergrowth, rifle ready.

Viper waited for him to pass, then approached silently from behind. A branch cracked.

The guy stopped and spun around.

Viper froze.

The guy peered into the darkness for a long moment, then slowly began to inch forward again.

Viper mirrored his movements, closing the gap a little more each time. Then, when the guy finally stopped, Viper sprang from the shadows and stabbed him in the neck. The mercenary's hand flew up to stem the bleeding, but Viper had hit the jugular. There was no coming back from this.

Slowly, the man sank to his knees, then dropped his hands to his sides and toppled forward. He'd hardly made a sound, other than the soft gargling as the life drained out of him. He'd never even seen his attacker.

"I'll take that," murmured Viper, picking up the guy's rifle. The CIA had only given them handguns, not semi-automatics. This would come in handy.

He covered the dead man with branches and continued forward, zigzagging to cover more ground. It wasn't long before he spotted another mercenary. This guy was big. Barrel-chested and thick-thighed, it would take more than one pounce to take him down.

He moved parallel to the merc, tracking him silently through the leaves. Despite being massive, the guy moved with a practiced grace. He was no stranger to jungle maneuvers.

He was fast too, pushing branches and foliage out of the way, but he wasn't particularly quiet. You could hear him coming a mile away. That was the downside of size.

When they were within fifty yards from where Izzy was hiding, Viper pounced. He jumped on the guy's back and tried to wrestle him to the ground. The big guy fell over, but not before he'd compressed the trigger and let out a short, but deafeningly loud, burst of fire.

Shit.

Now the rest of the tangos would come running.

He figured there was no point in being quiet now and shot the big guy in the head. He died instantly.

Viper pushed him away and got to his feet. There was blood spatter on his shirt. He had to get out of there. Even now, the jungle was being torn apart as men came crashing toward the sound of gunfire.

He knew Phoenix would come too. For the hunter always followed the hunted.

If used to their advantage, this could provide the diversion they needed to take out the pack.

He melted into the undergrowth and waited. Sure enough, three others appeared, crouching low, weapons drawn.

"Damn, Diego's down," one of them hissed in a low voice. He had a thick, rolling accent. Not Argentinian, but local. A lot of mercs working in Mexico were ex-military or cartel enforcers. They'd probably told Emily they were Argentinian as a cover, and she'd believed them. She had no reason not to.

"Was it them?" asked another.

"Yeah, I guess so. Be careful, man."

More grunts and the men spread out from Diego's position.

There was another short burst of fire from the other side and one of the men fell.

Phoenix.

Viper took out the one closest to him, then dived into the undergrowth for cover as the remaining merc opened fire. Bullets slammed into the trees above him.

More shooting and a yell as the third guy went down.

Viper popped his head up.

"Good job," he said, as Phoenix appeared out of the shadows.

"That's four down," said Viper.

"Five," Phoenix corrected. "I took one out with my knife."

One left to go.

The last kidnapper had obviously heard the commotion, but wisely kept himself hidden. Even now, he was probably tracking them.

Phoenix gave him a hand signal that meant, I'll double back. You go on.

Viper nodded.

It was so dark between the trees that anyone watching wouldn't have a clear shot unless they got up close and personal. And they wouldn't risk opening fire and giving away their position. Not when it was two against one.

So now the hunt began.

Viper set out, creeping through the undergrowth, his ears peeled.

Every now and then he thought he heard a rustle, but it could be anything. There were gangs operating in these jungles, hostile banditos armed with weapons. This was Mexico. Danger lurked around every corner.

He stopped, hunkered down and listened. The rustling continued for a while, then stopped. Definitely someone tracking him. He waited, willing them to show themselves. As soon as he got a visual, he could take them out. But the guy didn't appear. He was good. Patient. Well trained.

Then he heard a shout and his blood went cold. It was Phoenix's voice. He sprang out of hiding and surged through the bush. The remaining mercenary had Phoenix in a head-lock and was reaching for his knife. He was going to slit his throat.

Not on my watch!

Viper took but a moment to aim and then shot the guy in the head. It exploded, covering Phoenix in gunk.

"Jeez!" he muttered, leaping away.

The man fell to the ground behind him.

Phoenix took a moment to compose himself. "Thanks, buddy. I thought I was a goner there for a minute."

Viper grinned, but he could see Phoenix was shaken. "Nah, far from it. I had your six."

They headed back toward the ditch where they'd hidden Izzy. "I hope she didn't hear the shots and freak out," said Phoenix.

Viper shook his head. "Nah, she's tougher than she looks."

"Get to know her quite well, did you?"

"Sort of." He avoided his friend's gaze. "You can learn a lot by watching someone."

Phoenix nodded in agreement. "You sure can."

Observation was a crucial part of their SEAL training. Watching and waiting. Waiting for that perfect moment to strike, just like a sniper lying in wait for the ideal shot.

"She seems nice," said Phoenix, unwilling to let it go.

Visions of her taunting him in the swimming pool sprang to mind.

I need a man's opinion.

"Nice isn't the word I'd use to describe her." He resisted a smile. Feisty, independent, sexy as hell. Vulnerable too. Izzy was all those things. "She's tough, but she's a good person."

His instincts told him so. Every time she provoked him, every time she paraded around in front of him, he sensed the strong woman underneath. There'd been no hint of that pampered princess since they'd rescued her. She may be a social goddess, an influencer and mistress of her domain, but when things got rough, she was just another scared hostage.

They got within twenty meters of her hiding place when Phoenix held up a hand. They both crouched down into the undergrowth. Viper had heard it too. Voices, the crunching of foliage. Then a shout.

Followed closely by a scream.

He went cold.

Fuck.

"They've found her," Viper whispered urgently.

"Who's they?" hissed back Phoenix.

"I don't know. These aren't the guys from the ship."

Phoenix shook his head. "This must be a different crew."

That meant locals—and locals meant trouble.

Viper gestured to Phoenix that they move closer. They belly-crawled through the vegetation until they had eyes on Izzy. The rain decreased visibility further, so they had to get closer than they would have liked.

She was surrounded by at least a dozen young men holding a ragtag assortment of weapons. One in particular was shouting at her in Spanish.

"I don't understand?" she sobbed.

He threw his hands up in the air and another man took his place.

"Who are you?" His English was heavily accented but passable.

She was too terrified to answer.

The man gripped her shoulder and shook her. Viper clenched his jaw but remained still.

"I'm a tourist," she blurted out.

Good girl.

"A tourist? Here?" He laughed. "Nobody comes here on vacation."

He had a point.

"I was on a yacht, but we got attacked and came ashore. I'm lost."

He stared at her, then at the first man, who was clearly in charge. The rest stood around gaping at her through the rain that was getting heavier by the minute. It wasn't looking good.

Viper glanced at Phoenix whose expression told him he knew exactly how serious this situation was. There were too many of them to take on, they'd probably end up getting themselves killed.

In these instances, the best thing to do was to let things play out and wait for a better opportunity to rescue her.

Not great for Izzy, though. She was obviously terrified. Her eyes were huge, and she kept peering into the bushes like she expected them to come to her rescue. He wanted to, he really did, but he couldn't.

The leader barked a command and the interpreter said, "Who are you with?"

She hesitated.

Viper grimaced.

"No one. I'm alone."

The men laughed.

"Where is your man?" sneered the interpreter. "You didn't come into the jungle alone."

She looked wildly into the bushes. Phoenix lay a warning hand on his shoulder.

The leader hissed a warning and the men spun outwards, weapons drawn. They were smart. This was a territorial gang, used to defending their patch.

They may look ragged and poor, but appearances could be deceiving. Those semi-automatic rifles shot real bullets and these guys had probably been firing them since they were teenagers. Some of them didn't know much else besides violence and war.

The leader shouted into the jungle. He had a deep, growly voice backed up by enough raw aggression to make most men shiver. Viper didn't speak much Spanish, but the meaning was clear.

"¡Salgan ahora!"

Both Viper and Phoenix lay stock-still, camouflaged by the undergrowth and the penetrating darkness. The locals had no idea they were less than five meters away.

"We know you are there," said the interpreter, taking matters into his own hands. "Come out now."

The small army surrounding Izzy gripped their assault rifles, their heads roving like satellite beacons.

The leader said something and gripped Izzy by her hair. She yelped. "No, don't hurt me. Please."

Shit.

Viper glanced at Phoenix, his expression grim.

The man kicked her in the back of her legs, forcing her to her knees. He placed the rifle against her forehead.

"Show yourself," the interpreter called out. "Or we kill your woman."

CHAPTER 20

"No!" Izzy screamed.

She didn't want to die like this, out in the middle of the jungle. Just another American tourist killed in unknown territory. A statistic. Her body never recovered. Left to rot. How had it come to this?

Two days ago, she was sunning herself by a hotel swimming pool, teasing Viper to come and join her.

God, Viper.

Where was he now? Was he watching this?

How could he let them do this to her?

Or did those shots she'd heard earlier mean he was dead? Him and Phoenix?

A sob caught in her throat.

Surely, if he was here, he'd come and save her.

The leader of this crazy bunch had her by the hair. It hurt like hell. It felt like it was being pulled out of her head by the roots. Yet that was the least of her worries. The butt of the rifle felt cold against her forehead, colder than the rain dripping down her back. So much for the dry clothing. At any moment he could pull the trigger and end her life. Just like that, she'd cease to exist.

Oh, God, please don't let me die, she prayed.

Then she heard a rustle in the bushes. She strained her eyes, but it was so dark and wet, she could only make out the twisted shadows of the trees.

"Okay, I'm coming out. Don't shoot."

She sobbed in relief.

Viper!

He emerged from the undergrowth, his hands up. He was holding a rifle, which they quickly took from him.

"You are her man?" the interpreter said.

He glanced at Izzy and nodded.

Her man.

She liked the sound of that.

"Why are you here?"

"We're lost," he said, echoing her words. He must have heard her speaking to them, which meant he'd been there all the time. "We came ashore and got lost in the jungle."

They laughed again. The leader pointed to the gun, prompting the interpreter to ask, "Where you get the weapon?"

"Off a dead guy back there." He gestured behind him into the jungle. "I don't know who he is. I found him and took his rifle for protection."

Izzy knew that wasn't true.

And where was Phoenix? Was he dead or also hiding, watching them?

The interpreter relayed this to his boss, who barked a command and two of the men disappeared into the dark foliage. A short time later, they came back dragging a body with them.

She gasped. The man was missing half of his head.

"You did this?" The interpreter glanced from the corpse to Viper and back again.

He shook his head. "No, sir. It wasn't me."

"Who then?"

He shrugged. "I don't know."

Izzy stared at him. *Had* he done that?

She wasn't sorry the kidnapper was dead, but to die like that, in such a brutal fashion. She shivered. Was there ever an easy way to die? The gun was still pressed against her forehead. At least this would be quick, like that poor guy lying on the ground.

The men were studying Viper, trying to figure him out.

Despite the situation, he was surprisingly calm. His shoulders were relaxed, his face expressionless, except for his eyes, which were watchful and focused on the leader. He stood with his legs slightly apart, his tall frame steady and unwavering, his hands still above his head. He towered above all of them, and was almost double the breadth, but he was unarmed, and there was only one of him.

Versus twelve of them.

And Phoenix—if he was still alive.

Tears ran down her face. What hope did they have?

The muzzle dug into her head, halting her tears. She gasped, terrified he was going to pull the trigger.

"We don't believe you," said the interpreter. "Tell us what you are doing here. Who are you working for?"

She heard a roll of thunder in the distance. The storm was fast approaching.

"Nobody. I'm not working for anyone."

The man pulled harder on her hair. She cried out.

This was it. In a second, she'd feel a bullet enter her skull and then her head would look like that guy's.

Oh, God. She squeezed her eyes shut.

Please let it be quick.

Then there was a shout and he let go of her hair. She toppled over, unable to support herself. Looking up, she saw Phoenix had him in a headlock, a pistol pressed to his temple.

The other men were shouting and training their rifles on Phoenix, who was holding their leader in a vise-like grip.

"Drop your weapons!" Phoenix yelled.

They didn't know what to do. They aimed at Phoenix, and then turned to aim at Viper, and then her.

Viper's voice rose above the shouting.

"He said, drop your weapons!" He had a pistol and was leveling it at the interpreter. With their two top men incapacitated, the rest put down their weapons.

She sobbed with relief. They'd cut the head off the snake, and the body had withered and died.

"Izzy, get the rifle and come and stand behind me." Viper's voice was steady, but firm.

She struggled to her feet and looked around.

"Over there. Do it now, Izzy. And get behind me."

She picked up the gun, unsure of how to hold it. Was it loaded? Would it go off? She'd never even touched one before. Fumbling with it, she darted behind him.

Phoenix began to walk backward, still holding the boss by the neck, the gun flush against his head. "Move and he's dead," he threatened.

The men stared at them, edgy and nervous. The rain was fast becoming a deluge. It dripped off their faces and pooled at their feet. At any moment all hell could break loose. Izzy just wanted to get out of there as quickly as possible.

"We are no threat to you," said Viper, his gun still pointed at the interpreter. "You let us go, and we'll leave you alone. Understand?"

He nodded.

"Tell them."

The interpreter did as he was told.

Phoenix came around to where they were standing, still holding the leader in a head lock. They backed into the undergrowth until they were out of sight of the gang.

"Keep going," murmured Viper. The men up ahead hadn't moved.

When they got about ten meters out, Phoenix brought the butt of his pistol down on the leader's head with enough force that he crumpled to the ground.

"Is he dead?" Izzy asked. He'd gone down like a sack of potatoes.

"No, but he'll have a sore head when he wakes up," muttered Phoenix. "Come on, let's get the hell out of here."

They turned and ran. She clutched Viper's hand they raced through the jungle back toward the beach. How they knew which direction to go in, she had no idea. All she could see was a dark mesh of dripping, tangled trees and bushes.

Still, somehow they made it, and twenty minutes later they emerged onto the wet sand.

"Thank God," gasped Izzy, as her shoes sunk into the sand.

The two men grabbed their inflatable from where they'd left it and dragged it back down to the sea. "Let's try further up the coast," Viper said, as they shoved it into the shallows. The storm had made landfall further to the south, so they'd only caught the tail end. Even now, the rain was abating.

She climbed in, her legs shaky, then collapsed onto the base of the boat.

Phoenix started the engine while Viper pushed the boat out into the shallows. When it was deep enough, he hopped in.

Izzy, unable to help herself, burst into tears. She couldn't help it.

Viper scooped her off the floor and placed her on the seat next to him. "You're safe now. There's no need to cry."

She heard his words but couldn't stop. "I'm just so happy to be alive."

"I know. You're in shock but try to relax. Everything's going to be okay."

She buried her head in his shoulder and hung on to him as Phoenix propelled the inflatable through the waves.

Would it? Would it be okay?

They had no idea who had kidnapped her, or why. She took some deep breaths and tried to calm herself. She was alive, that was the main thing. She hadn't been shot in the jungle. Thanks to Viper and Phoenix, she was safe.

For now.

CHAPTER 21

*V*iper held her close until she stopped crying. She felt so good in his arms, goddamn it. Better than she should, given the circumstances. He stroked her hair and whispered that everything was going to be all right.

She clung to him, her arm wrapped around his waist, her face buried in his chest. A shadow of the confident, cocky woman she'd been in San Diego. A wave of possessiveness like he'd never known swept over him. All he wanted to do was kiss away her fear and make her smile again.

Fucking hell. She'd really gotten under his skin.

He tried to tell himself this was a once-off, a bad experience that she'd forget in time, just like she'd forget about him, but it wasn't working. Right now, feeling her trembling beside him, all he wanted to do was envelope her in his arms and keep her safe.

Phoenix drove like the wind, parallel to the shore and away from the storm. The gang didn't follow. They weren't willing to risk their lives for the sake of three strangers. Wise move.

"We've got less than a quarter of a tank," Phoenix warned, glancing at the gauge. "We're going to have to go in soon."

"Take us up the coast as far as you can." Viper watched the endless stretch of jungle go by. As they headed north, it gradually gave way to patches of palms and then to more arid scrubland. The coastline was becoming more developed with occasional signs of human habitation.

"What's that?" Phoenix pointed ahead to the shore.

Viper squinted through the darkness. Years of practice had fine-tuned his night vision. "It looks like some sort of resort. Those are lounge chairs on the beach."

Izzy raised her head. "And folded up umbrellas. It is a resort!"

There was no mistaking the relief in her voice.

Phoenix angled the boat toward the shore. Izzy watched eagerly as they got ever closer.

"Hold on," warned Viper, as Phoenix climbed the back of a wave. "It's going to get bumpy."

She gripped the guard rope, her other arm still around his waist, and hung on as they flew over the crest and into the trough. Once again, the momentum shot the inflatable forward and they surfed the whitewater into the beach.

It was quiet and calm as they pulled the boat up onto the sand. The canvas of night was dotted with stars that sparkled down on them, oblivious to the traumatic events that had taken place far below.

"Looks like we might be able to give the CIA their boat back, after all," Phoenix said, making him smile.

Viper helped Izzy out of the boat. She stumbled, her legs shaky.

"You okay?"

She gave a little nod but clutched his hand like she was afraid to let go. This needy, clingy Izzy didn't fit with the feisty, independent woman he'd gotten to know these last few days. But then, she'd had a shock.

Truth be told, he didn't mind. He liked having her close to him, her hand buried in his, even if it was making him think things he shouldn't. Once they were inside and surrounded by managers and staff and normality, she'd revert back to her normal self. He was sure about that.

It might be wrong, it might be unprofessional, but he didn't let it go. Phoenix shot him an inquisitive look as they strode up the beach. He shrugged and kept walking, enjoying the feel of her soft hand in his big, calloused one.

They walked through the hotel's landscaped gardens. Toward the east, far beyond the hotel, the black sky was dissolving into indigo. Viper reckoned sunrise was still an hour off.

They rounded an azure-blue swimming pool, lit up by underwater lights. It looked warm and inviting. There was no breeze and the humidity clung to them like a blanket.

Izzy eyed it longingly.

"Let's get settled in first." Viper didn't think he could stand to see her floating in the pool right now. Not without taking her into his arms and kissing the fear and anxiety away. The memory of her breasts bobbing on the water hadn't left him, nor the sight of her perfectly rounded behind, or those endless legs.

The night manager gaped when they walked in. Viper couldn't blame him. They must look a sight. Their clothes were wet, and covered with dirty and grime, while he had the addition of a faint spray of red mist.

Phoenix was far worse. He had a cut on his neck from where one of the kidnappers had nicked him with a knife, and his T-shirt and the side of his neck were splattered with dried clots of blood that had turned a dark brown. Izzy, in her jeans and his sweatshirt, looked the most normal, even if it was several sizes too big for her.

"You are hurt!" cried the night manager, rushing forward to tend to Phoenix.

"It's not my blood," muttered Phoenix, which caused even more consternation.

Viper elbowed him in the ribs.

Izzy let go of his hand. "Good evening," she said in her poshest voice.

Immediately the night manager stood up straight and turned to face her.

"Good evening, Ma'am."

"I'm sorry for arriving in this disheveled state," she began. "We encountered some trouble in the jungle and were robbed. We're okay," she said hurriedly, holding up a hand as his face showed concern. "We managed to get away. But could we please have two rooms? We'll contact the authorities in the morning."

Two rooms.

Viper avoided Phoenix's gaze.

She was right. He needed to stay close to her. The people who'd tried to kidnap her might try again. It wouldn't take long to figure out that they must have gone north along the coast. There wasn't anywhere else to go. While she was a target, it was his job to keep her safe. If that meant sleeping in her room, so be it.

"Of course, ma'am. I'll see to it immediately." He darted back behind the desk and began typing into the computer. "Your names?" he asked, gazing from Izzy to them and back again.

She hesitated, then said, "Victoria Granger."

Viper arched a brow, impressed by her fast thinking. Phoenix was nodding too. It was smart not checking in under her own name. "My husband is going to pay for it," she smiled, and gestured to Viper.

Phoenix made a coughing noise in the back of his throat.

Viper stepped forward. "Viper Morgan." He handed over the credit card he kept for emergencies. It was always zipped into the side pocket of his cargo pants. Nothing would shake it loose, not even a dip in the ocean.

Two minutes later they were handed keycards to their rooms.

"202 and 204," the night manager said. "They're adjacent to each other on the second floor. Breakfast is served from seven to nine a.m." He glanced tiredly at his watch. "In two hours' time."

Izzy gave a curt nod. "Thank you."

"Nicely done." Phoenix grinned at Izzy as they walked toward the elevator.

She flushed. "The accent comes in handy sometimes."

Phoenix glanced between the two of them. "Husband and wife, huh?"

Izzy shrugged. "I thought it best. I don't want anyone to think I'm alone. Not here, not anymore." She glanced at Viper. "You don't mind, do you? After what's happened, I—"

"I don't mind," he said gruffly. "It's a good idea."

She nodded.

Phoenix didn't comment.

"How about we get some shuteye and regroup in a couple of hours? Say ten o'clock?" Phoenix suggested, once they got to their rooms.

Viper could barely keep his eyes open. He could count the number of hours sleep he'd had since Izzy was kidnapped on one hand. "Roger that."

Izzy paused, before she unlocked the door. "Thanks for saving me." She looked at both of them. "I don't know what I would have done if you hadn't come to get me."

"Don't mention it," Phoenix said. "Besides, Pat would have killed us if we hadn't."

That made her laugh, and Viper was pleased to see her face light up, even if it was just for a moment. A glimpse of the old Izzy. "He can be pretty scary, can't he?"

Phoenix grimaced. "You have no idea."

"We should let him know you're safe," Viper said.

Phoenix nodded. "I'll take care of it."

Viper nodded his thanks. He hoped to hell that getting Izzy back would redeem him in the eyes of the former SEAL Commander, who would let him keep his job.

CHAPTER 22

Izzy walked into the hotel room and flopped down on the bed. "I'm so exhausted, I can hardly move." She caught a whiff of herself and frowned. Saltwater, adrenaline, sweat, fear, and dirt clung to her like an unwelcome second skin. "But first, I need to take a shower."

"I'll go after you," Viper said, his voice tense.

He hadn't looked her in the eye since she'd booked the two rooms. The awkwardness was palpable, more so than the fatigue weighing her down. Up until now, they'd always had adjoining rooms. He'd been next door, a shout away if she needed him.

God, how she'd taunted him, calling him to help her choose an outfit. It seemed ridiculous now, in light of all that had happened.

Still, she didn't regret her decision. She was keeping him close to her until this fiasco with the mine was over.

"I'm sorry about what's happened," she said suddenly.

He frowned. "It's not your fault."

"Well, it sort of is. It's my inheritance that's causing all this trouble. That's why they're coming after me. You didn't ask for any of this. You and Phoenix nearly got killed because of me."

"Actually, I did ask for it." He took a step closer, his presence overwhelming. "That's my job. It's what I'm trained to do."

She digested that. "Okay," she admitted with a thin smile. "I suppose it is."

They stared at each other for a long moment. Despite her exhaustion, her pulse raced like the inflatable boat they'd left on the beach.

"Thank you," she blurted out. "For saving me. Twice."

He gave an embarrassed nod. "Like I said, Miss Beaumont, I was only doing my job. This is exactly why you hired me."

She couldn't work him out. The gentle giant was gone, replaced by a controlled, polite demeanor that irked her so much she'd made a fool of herself trying to budge it.

"Why do you do that?" she asked.

"What?" His blue-green eyes flickered. In the hotel light, they looked like the water in the swimming pool.

"Act so distant."

He looked confused. "I'm being professional."

She sighed. "I think we're past that, don't you?"

He didn't respond, just gazed at her, deep and blue.

She put a hand on his chest. His heart beat slow and steady, not racing like hers. "Please call me Izzy." He had done so in the jungle, when it had meant something.

A flicker of a smile. Another tiny nod. He reached into his pocket. "This belongs to you."

She gasped. "My necklace! How did you—?"

"I picked it up off the deck of the yacht," he said. "The night you were taken."

"Thank you." She took the pendant and stared at it. "I can't believe you found it."

"You're welcome." He turned away.

Still in a daze, Izzy took herself off to the bathroom. When she got back, Viper was standing topless in the middle of the room, his shirt discarded on the floor. She gazed at his sculpted, godlike torso, unable to peel her eyes away.

"It was covered in blood," he said, by way of explanation.

She nodded and walked past him to the bed. She wore a fluffy robe she'd found hanging behind the bathroom door. It felt blissful after her damp, dirty clothes. "I don't have anything to wear." She gestured to the robe.

"We'll sort something out tomorrow." He strode toward the bathroom, hardly looking at her.

She sighed. This took awkward to a new level.

But what was she supposed to do? She was terrified of being alone. He'd made her feel so safe on the boat, holding her in his muscular arms, warming her with his powerful body. She wanted to feel that again.

Pulling back the covers, she climbed into bed. Her whole life she'd been on her own. Her mother had passed away when she was in her teens, and after that, her workaholic father had put her in boarding school. She'd seen him on holidays, but he'd always been in some exotic corner of the world, and soon she'd opted to stay with friends rather than travel to Mexico to see him. It had been her against the world.

Then Viper had appeared, and while she didn't want a bodyguard, she had to admit, it felt good knowing he was always there, looking out for her. She'd never had that before.

Then, that moment on the boat. For the first time in her life, she'd felt well and truly protected. Safe. Like nothing could touch her. It was addictive.

Viper emerged from the bathroom in the second robe, part of his tattoo visible where the material met over his chest, a puff of steam billowing out behind him. With his hair slicked back, his rugged, tanned face and piercing aquamarine eyes that looked everywhere but at her, he was Neptune incarnate.

"I'll sleep on the floor," he said gruffly.

"Don't be silly. This bed is big enough for the both of us. It's only for a few hours, then we're going to go home, right?" He hesitated. She could tell he was on the point of refusing.

"Please, I feel bad letting you sleep on the floor after all you've done for me. I wouldn't have gotten us one room if I'd known you were going to do that."

He gave in and sat down on the bed, his back to her.

She smiled.

"You should call Robert," he muttered. "He'll be worried."

"Shoot, I forgot. You're right. They'll be frantic."

Viper didn't reply.

She picked up the hotel phone and dialed a number from memory.

Nothing between them. Yeah, right.

"Robert, it's me."

"Izzy, thank God. I've been so worried. We all have. Are you okay? Where the hell are you? Tell me, I'll send someone to get you."

"I'm fine, Robert. Don't worry. Please tell Emily I'm okay."

"But where are you?"

"I—I'm not sure. Mexico, I think."

"Jesus Christ, what are you doing there?"

"The fishing trawler brought me here. But Viper and Phoenix rescued me."

"Viper? The bodyguard?" She heard the incredulousness in his voice, along with more than a touch of irritation.

"Yes. I just wanted to let you know I'm safe. I'll call you in the morning."

"Wait! Izzy, where are you now?"

"I'm tired, Rob. I have to go, but I'll call you back in a couple of hours. Don't forget to tell Emily I'm okay." And she cut him off.

"You didn't tell him where you were?" Viper held her hostage with his eyes, probing.

She shook her head. "No way, I didn't want him sending a SWAT team after me. Robert always goes a bit overboard when it comes to me." She smiled softly. "I'm safe here with you and Phoenix. We'll have plenty of time to answer questions once we're back home."

He didn't immediately respond, just looked at her thoughtfully. She was too tired to try to decipher his thoughts.

"Let's get some sleep," she said.

He lay down next to her. Heat radiated off him, along with a clean, masculine scent that stirred her senses.

He switched off the light, plunging the room into darkness. The heavy drapes blocked out the encroaching dawn.

"Viper?" she whispered.

"Yes." He didn't move.

"Will you hold me?"

Silence.

"Please," she pleaded. "Hold me like you did on the boat."

Without waiting for him to reply, she shuffled over and rested her head on his chest. His robe had fallen open and a smattering of chest hair tickled her cheek.

He felt so good.

She wrapped her arm over his stomach, rock-solid beneath the robe, and snuggled up to him. After a long moment, he adjusted his arm and wrapped it around her.

She sighed. This was perfect. Just what she needed.

Within seconds, she'd fallen asleep.

CHAPTER 23

*V*iper held Izzy as she slept and tried to relax, but it was downright impossible. Her damp hair tickled his chest, soft and golden. She smelled wonderful, fresh and clean, and he wanted so much to kiss her.

She was snuggled into him the way a girlfriend might, her arm loosely draped over his stomach, her leg over his. It was perfect.

It was torture.

He'd rather face a night of waterboarding than endure this.

What the hell was he thinking?

He'd crossed just about every line he could think of. The principal-bodyguard line, the employer-employee line—not to mention his normal stance on relationships.

His body had instantly reacted to the contact, and even now, he could see the covers tenting over his massive hard-on. Luckily, Izzy was dead to the world and hadn't noticed.

Her breathing was even and rhythmic, unlike his shallow and labored breaths.

Goddamn.

He couldn't even move to massage himself, to relieve the ache. So, he lay there, perfectly still and pretended he was holed up behind enemy lines. Camouflaged in a forward operating post, unable to move. He forced his mind to go blank, like he used to in those situations, and focused on his breathing. Soon, it slowed, and his arousal faded. Grogginess descended and the exhaustion of the last few days returned. He felt himself drifting, and eventually, he fell asleep.

THE TELEPHONE RANG, waking him with a start.

What the hell?

The room was still dark and he was momentarily confused. Then it came flooding back in a rush. The jungle... the race up the coast... the resort... the double bed.

Her...

He glanced down at the sleeping figure still wrapped around him. She stirred, then snuggled some more.

He patted her shoulder. "Izzy, the phone's ringing."

She murmured something unintelligible and snuggled deeper. Her hand slipped under his robe, splaying across his abs.

He froze. What was she playing at?

It snaked up to his chest, her fingers grazing his chest hair. His body was on fire. Christ, he was harder than the Washington Monument.

She opened her eyes and mumbled, "You get it."

He sat up and reached for the phone.

She shifted off him and lay on her side, watching, her eyes dark and huge.

"Hello?"

"It's me. I hope you're decent; I'm coming over. I've just spoken to Pat."

"Right, see you now." Viper shot out of bed, fastening his robe. "Phoenix is coming over."

Izzy groaned. "Now?"

"Yep, he's heard from Pat."

He opened the blind and lifted the window, letting in some fresh air. It was mid-morning, the sun high in the sky.

"Okay." She gave him a lingering glance, then got up and disappeared to the bathroom.

A moment later, there was a knock on the door.

"Hey, buddy." Phoenix bounded in. His gaze fell on the bed. "How did you sleep?"

Viper didn't miss the cheeky sparkle.

"Fine, thank you. What did Pat have to say?"

Phoenix chuckled. "He was overjoyed we got Izzy back. He's very fond of her, from what I can gather."

"Yeah, she's his goddaughter," Viper told him.

"Shit, really? He kept that quiet. Anyway, they've managed to trace the registered owners of the *Pacific Pride* to a shell company in El Salvador. Get this, the shell company is registered to a man affiliated with La Sombra Roja."

"Thought so," muttered Viper. "I recognized them from the hotel in San Diego."

"Emily's friends?" gasped Izzy, emerging from the bathroom.

Viper gave a slim nod. "Seems so. I'm sorry. That's how they knew you were going to be on the yacht."

"Em told them?" Her eyes were huge.

"Inadvertently," Viper said, hastily.

Izzy sank down onto the bed. "I didn't suspect them for a moment."

Viper ground his jaw. "Nobody did." Including him.

"What if we stayed here for a while?" Izzy said, softly.

Viper and Phoenix both looked at her.

"It's not a bad idea," Phoenix said, after a pause.

Viper felt a knot tighten in his stomach. "We're in the middle of nowhere."

"Exactly. Nobody knows I'm here," Izzy insisted, warming to her plan. "I didn't tell Robert, Pat won't mention anything, not even the police or FBI knows where we are. If the guys who kidnapped me are all dead, they can't tell the cartel where we are. Even when they realize what's happened, they'll assume we're long gone."

"They might check the coastal hotels," Viper said, thinking that's what he'd do.

"They won't expect you to stick around," Phoenix pointed out. "I think Izzy's right. The longer you stay holed up here the better. I'll go back to D.C., and we'll keep looking into who's behind this. In the meantime, you two sit tight."

"We'll have to run it by Pat," Viper said. He couldn't look at Izzy. He didn't want to see her wide eyes staring up at him.

Will you hold me?

Christ.

"I don't want this on my credit card," he muttered.

Phoenix chuckled. "Don't worry, we'll sort that out. In the meantime, I need some decent clothes to wear before I leave for the airport. I can't catch a flight like this."

"That I can help you with." Izzy reached for the phone. "There's a vacation shop downstairs in the lobby. It looks like it sells clothes."

"You noticed that last night?" said Phoenix, astonished. "And here I thought I was observant."

"You're trained to notice terrorist threats and men with guns. I'm trained to notice retail."

Viper chortled.

She turned to the phone. "This is Victoria Granger, Room 202. Could you please put me through to the shop in the hotel lobby?"

The men listened as she reeled off their sizes and told the shop manager what they required.

Izzy grinned at them. "She'll be up in fifteen minutes with some samples."

"Good guess." Viper was impressed by how easily she'd sized them up.

"Well, that's sorted then," grinned Phoenix. "I know who to get to do my shopping for me, in future."

"It is what I do," Izzy said with a laugh. "I can't vouch for the quality of the clothes, but at least you'll be able to go outside."

"I'm starving." Phoenix picked up a room service menu. "Let's eat and then I'll call a cab to take me to the airport."

They ordered three cheeseburgers with fries and got three Cokes out of the fridge. After they were done, the store manager arrived with bags of samples, which she proceeded to lay out on the bed.

Izzy picked out two summer dresses with bright floral patterns—one was short, ending above the knee, and the other was a long, flowy maxi dress. She held them up and smiled. "These are perfect."

She also grabbed a pair of sandals and some flip-flops.

Viper wavered, and she could tell these beach clothes weren't his style. Eventually, and only because he had no other choice, he selected a pair of shorts and two T-shirts, one with a sombrero on it and the other a dolphin. It was the only thing in extra-large. Phoenix chose a pair of white Bermuda shorts and a Hawaiian-style shirt with peppers and cacti in crazy colors all over it. Both men had to settle for leather sandals, as all the closed shoes were too small for them.

"You won't win any style awards, but you'll do," Izzy said, trying not to giggle at how different they looked.

Dressed in his multicolor ensemble, Phoenix said, "Okay,

folks. I'm going to leave you to it and make my way to the airport."

"How far away is it?" Izzy asked.

He shrugged. "I have no idea, but I'm sure the helpful concierge will point me in the right direction. See ya back in D.C." He gave Viper a handshake turned shoulder-bump and gave Izzy a quick hug. "You two take care now."

"We will."

Phoenix caught Viper's eye and grinned. "You can trust Viper. He'll take good care of you."

CHAPTER 24

*I*zzy sat under an umbrella and read a romance novel bought in the resort gift shop. It was the only thing she could find in English. She'd also purchased a swimsuit and a pair of swimming trunks for Viper. Now that they were away from everybody, there was no reason why he couldn't join her in the pool.

Shamefully, she couldn't wait to see him out of those clothes. The tiny glimpses she'd had of his bare torso had stunned her, and part of her just wanted to see if it really was as gorgeous as she remembered.

He'd felt secure enough to leave her sunning herself while he went to sort out the inflatable. He'd told her it belonged to the CIA, and he wanted to send it back. Izzy took a deep breath. If he wasn't worried, then neither was she.

Not really.

Although, she did keep glancing at her fellow guests, wondering if they were really who they seemed to be.

The resort wasn't busy, and she was one of three women lying by the pool. There appeared to be a conference in the convention center attached to the hotel, and the lobby was filled with flashy men in expensive suits and well-coiffed women in designer outfits, expensive shoes, and expertly manicured nails. What could she say? She noticed these things.

Izzy read her book and tried to remain unobtrusive. She wore a cheap pair of sunglasses and stayed on the lounge chair, getting up only to take a dip in the swimming pool when she needed to cool off. The less attention she drew to herself, the better.

It was strange not having a phone or laptop with her. Usually, she was joined to both at the hip, and now she didn't have them, it took some getting used to. She wondered if Emily had pushed on with the fashion shoot or whether they'd abandoned it until she got back.

She was dying to ring her assistant but knew that was out of the question. Viper had told her explicitly not to call anyone, and for once, she was going to listen to him.

"ALL SET." Viper appeared from the path that led down to the beach. He had sand on his feet and was wiping his hands on his T-shirt with the dolphin on it.

She smiled. "You look like you've just gotten back from a day at the beach."

That hint of a dimple. "I have."

"Nobody would ever guess you were my bodyguard."

He sat down beside her on an empty lounger. "That's a good thing. The less conspicuous we are, the better. It helps if people think we're a couple."

If only they were.

She couldn't meet his gaze for fear he'd see right through her, see her yearning, the desire that had been building ever since she'd first met him.

"The newspapers are full of your disappearance," he said, his voice edged with concern.

"They are?" The thought pulled her roughly back to reality.

"Yeah, I spoke to Blade earlier. Your abduction caused quite a stir. Your social media's been blowing up. Everyone's asking if you're okay."

"Crap, I should reply." She bit her lip, anxiously. "You can't ignore your followers. They can be so fickle—think you don't care, and they'll move on in a heartbeat."

He shook his head. "I'm not sure that's wise."

"Okay, fine, but I have to speak to Emily. She needs to release a statement that I'm okay and thank them for their concern. It's imperative. This is my business, Viper."

His nod was curt. "Call Emily from reception, but don't tell her where you're staying."

She pursed her lips. "I don't think I even know the name of this hotel."

He snorted. "Let's keep it that way."

She got up and handed him the swimming trunks. "I got these for you. I thought you might like to jump in." She nodded at the pool. "The water's amazing."

"Thanks, but maybe later." Now it was his turn to avoid her gaze. She wondered what he was thinking, why he was so resistant to enjoying himself with her?

"You aren't on duty all the time, you know," she told him. "Just being with me is enough. You said yourself, we're safe here."

"I know." He walked beside her into the lobby. "But it's complicated. I've already fucked up once. I can't afford to do it again."

"Having a swim is not fucking up. You deserve a little down time."

He stared straight ahead. "Make your call and then, maybe, we can go for a swim."

She grinned. "Deal."

Emily was ecstatic to hear from her and gabbled on for a full five minutes about how worried she was and how she hadn't been sleeping and thank God Izzy was all right.

"Emily, I need you to issue a press release," Izzy interrupted gently.

Emily gulped and calmed down. "Okay, sorry. Shoot."

"Tell my followers that I'm okay and thanks for their concern. Say I'm taking a break from the public eye for a short while, but I'll be back soon. Post some of the photographs Max took of me in San Diego. There are some good ones there. They'll think I'm still on vacation somewhere, recuperating."

"You are okay, aren't you?" Emily's voice wobbled with concern.

"Yes, don't worry. I'm fine. I'm with Viper."

"Oh?"

"Not like that. He's protecting me." Saying it didn't stop the excited flutter she felt in her stomach.

Emily sniffed. "As long as you're all right, I don't care who you're with. Text me if you need anything."

"I can't. My phone is at the bottom of the ocean right now. But I'll call you if there's anything else. Oh, did you finish the shoot?"

"Yes, I thought you'd want to get it done while we had the crew out there. Was that the right thing to do?" She sounded guilty. "I thought about canceling it, but it was only the catalog shoot which we didn't really need you for, and I didn't want to waste money, especially since we'd paid everyone up front."

"You did the right thing," she confirmed, her voice warm. "Thanks, Em. You're the best."

They talked for a few minutes longer, then Izzy said goodbye, and handed the receiver back to the concierge. "I feel better now that's taken care of," she said as they made their way back up to the room. "I can't afford to let my followers wane. As it is, I'll have to explain to my sponsors why I'm not advertising this week. Luckily, I had planned on taking a week off anyway, so they were expecting it."

Viper opened the door, then stuck his head in to check out the room before she entered. Always on the lookout. "I get it. Your contracts depend on their support."

When it was safe, she followed him in. "Exactly."

"I'll just get changed." Viper made sure the door was locked behind them, then headed for the bathroom. With only the one room between them, the bathroom offered the only privacy.

Izzy was so *not* prepared for how he looked when he emerged a few moments later.

Whoa!

That gorgeous body, perfectly honed, a smattering of chest hair, military ink over a bulging pectoral and... Holy crap! The swim trunks were on the small size, leaving pretty much nothing to the imagination.

"Oh," she stammered, eyes wide and failing miserably to look away. "I'm sorry, that was the biggest size they had."

"It's okay. They're fine."

She sure as hell wasn't complaining.

He turned his back on her and she gasped, noticing the two coarse, circular scars on his back. One was positioned above his shoulder blade, the other on his right side below his ribs. "Are those...bullet wounds?"

Viper reached for his shirt and pulled it on. "Yeah, happened a couple of months back."

"You were shot?"

He grimaced. "Occupational hazard." His tone told her he

didn't want to talk about it. She watched as he pulled on the shorts, then picked up the towel, slotting his gun between the folds.

Scarred hands. Bullet wounds. Firearm. His life was so different from hers. Filled with violence and death.

Yet, he was also so gentle. The way he'd held her...

"Ready?" He cut into her thoughts.

Slightly breathless, she picked up her towel and followed him out of the room.

The swimming pool and surrounding terrace was deserted, everybody else having left, so they had the whole place to themselves.

"This is even better than San Diego," Izzy called, as she slipped into the water. As earlier, it was still the perfect temperature. Warm and caressing, and totally relaxing.

"It's a lot more private," he agreed, his midnight gaze fixed on her.

She leaned against the edge of the pool. "You coming in?"

Viper carefully placed his towel on the lounger, then, with a confident stride, he walked around to the deep end and dove in.

She watched, mesmerized, as he swum toward her. His powerful strokes sliced through the water, creating hardly a ripple. When he stood up, water cascading off his broad shoulders, her mouth went dry.

There were no words.

He grinned at her. "You were right, this is great."

Her heart lurched at the relaxed, carefree expression on his face. It was the happiest she'd ever seen him. "You like the water, don't you?"

"Love it. That's why I joined the SEALs."

Izzy's gaze fell to the intricate design of his tattoo. It was the first chance she'd had to really study it up close. A fierce eagle with its wings spread wide, clutching a U.S. Navy anchor, a flintlock-style pistol, and a trident. The detailed lines and shading of the tattoo highlighted the eagle's feathers and the sharp edges of the trident. "I didn't know you were a Navy SEAL."

He blinked, as if realizing what he'd said. "Yeah, that's where I met Phoenix, on the SEAL training course."

She exhaled, the pieces clicking into place. The rescue, the precision, the ease with which they'd extracted her and brought her here. "Pat didn't say."

He shrugged, the movement causing small waves around them. "We don't usually talk about it, but I guess it's okay, since I'm out. Most of the guys your uncle hires are ex-special ops. That's why they have such a good track record."

"Except for me." She rolled her eyes. "I was a failed operation."

He took a step toward her. "We got you back. No harm done."

"True." She sobered, the weight of their situation pressing down. "Do you think we'll ever catch who's doing this?"

"Pat and the rest of the unit are very good," he said, after a short pause. "If anyone can figure it out, it'll be them."

"I hope so," she breathed. "I don't want to live in fear my entire life."

"It won't be like that," he reassured her, his voice firm. "We'll get to the bottom of it. You'll get your old life back. Don't worry."

Izzy fell silent, content to float gently. The calm of the pool contrasted sharply with the chaos they'd left behind. Viper did the same, treading water in the deep end. She could feel the water moving outwards around him, caressing her.

"This is a nice change," she murmured, after a brief pause. "Not having a million people around. No phone beeping. No emails to respond to. It feels surreal."

"Enjoy it while you can. All too soon it'll go back to normal," he said, then turned on his back and kicked down the length of the pool.

She watched as he swam toward her, admiring the way the water glisten on his smooth, tanned shoulders. The muscles rippled as he moved, and she unable to help herself, she followed the line of his washboard abs down to where they disappeared beneath the water. "How long were you in the Navy SEALs?"

He was silent for a moment. "Almost seven years," he said finally.

"Why'd you quit?"

"I got shot."

She hesitated. "The marks on your back?"

"Yeah. And another in the thigh. After I got out of the hospital, they declared me unfit for duty. I never went back." His face looked so stricken she wanted to reach out to him, to comfort him.

"I'm sorry," she whispered.

He shrugged, but she could see it still bothered him.

"Do you miss it?"

He nodded, the water rippling around him.

"So, you've gone from that to me?"

He managed a weak smile. "It could be worse. I could be guarding some boring diplomat in the Middle East."

"Instead, you're hiding out at a luxury resort in Mexico." She burst out laughing, the sound echoing off the water. "Crazy, right?"

"It's not what I expected." He smiled at her, the tension easing from his face. "But I'm glad I was here when it counted."

She grew serious, the laughter dying on her lips. "Me too."

The water seemed to sizzle between them. Slowly, she swam toward him, drawn in by the intensity of his gaze, the same color as the water around them. Looping her arms around his neck, she looked deep into his eyes. "You don't mind, do you?"

He shook his head, his gaze never leaving hers. No words, just those eyes burning into hers.

Tentatively, she stood on her tiptoes, her lips brushing his. At first, she thought he wasn't going to respond, but then his powerful arms wrapped around her waist and pulled her firmly against him.

CHAPTER 25

The moment Izzy's lips locked with his, Viper knew he was in trouble. Seething desire raged through his blood, igniting the feelings he'd tried to bury this whole time. This woman had upended his entire world, and now she was in his arms, kissing him like he'd only fantasized about.

He shoved aside all the reasons why he shouldn't be doing this and wrapped his arms around her, pulling her close, kissing her hard. He delved into her mouth, exploring her, tasting her, devouring her.

She gasped at the sudden power shift, then reciprocated, matching his passion with her own. Her arms around his neck tightened, and her legs wrapped around him under the water, anchoring her body to his.

Fuck, she felt amazing. Her breasts were crushed against his chest, her smooth stomach rubbed against his, and her long legs gripped the back of his calves. It was the hottest kiss he could remember. Ever. He didn't want to let go, didn't want it to end.

The water lapped around them as the kiss deepened.

They hungrily explored each other's mouths, tasting and savoring as if they'd been starved and were finally allowed to indulge.

Her skin was soft and slid against his under the water, making it all the more erotic. His cock got the message and sprang to life, straining painfully against the swimming trunks. She locked her legs around him, making him groan. The heat in his balls and the coolness of the water was driving him crazy. Add to that the gentle rubbing of her groin, and he was ready to explode.

He still hadn't stopped kissing her. Couldn't. She was addictive, like water when you'd been stuck in the Afghan desert for weeks. He drank her in, losing himself in her kiss. Drowning.

Holy Christ. He was losing it.

She clung to him like a limpet, heat radiating between them. Grasping her butt, crushing her against his throbbing erection, he wouldn't have been surprised to see the fucking water boiling.

Izzy moaned his name and, swear to God, he got goosebumps. Somehow, she repositioned herself so that his cock was rubbing against the lycra fabric of her bathing suit. He felt her softness, her heat, and nearly came right then and there.

He had to get a grip. He couldn't let rip in the goddamn swimming pool, no matter how badly he wanted to.

But hell, if only the material wasn't there. He was desperate to be inside her, to feel her heat, to claim her as his own.

But he mustn't. Jesus, he must not.

That would be impossible to come back from. A heated kiss in the swimming pool on a hot day was explainable, justifiable even. But sex?

No one ever came back from sex. Not on a job.

It would ruin everything.

He began to push her away, but she clung to him, her voice hoarse with desire. She was feeling it too. "Don't stop."

"Izzy, I—"

She reached under the water and pulled down his trunks, followed by her own, which she kicked off. They floated to the surface behind her.

"We can't…" he whispered.

She held his gaze, her eyes filled with a heat that had his heart pounding faster than a semi-automatic. "We can."

Suddenly, there was nothing between them anymore. The cool water caressed his cock before she wrapped herself around him again.

This time he was lost. A loud groan escaped him as he plunged into her deep, dark depths.

Oh, shit.

He froze, wondering if it was a mistake, but she ground against him, urging him on.

After that, he couldn't stop himself. He bit down on her lip as he thrust inside. She gasped and hung onto him like a life raft in stormy seas. Like she had in the inflatable.

Her fingertips pressed into his back, and she cried, "Oh!" before finding his mouth again.

He held her butt firm and began to move in and out of her, slowly and luxuriously, savoring every stroke.

Fuck.

He'd never felt anything like it.

Her bikini top came undone and floated away. Her nipples grazed his chest, hard now from her arousal and the temperature of the water.

He kissed her hard and deep until she broke away, gasping for breath.

"Oh, God, Viper. Feels. So. Good."

He captured her mocha gaze and saw everything he was

feeling mirrored there. A desperate desire that neither of them could hide any longer. She wanted this as much as he did.

They picked up the rhythm, eyes locked on each other. Viper found he was too scared to look away in case it broke the spell, but he was terrified that if he maintained eye contact, he'd betray himself and she'd see how he really felt about her.

The water rippled around them, slapping against the sides of the pool. Luckily, there was no one about, although he probably wouldn't care at this point, even if there was.

He drove into her until she gasped and flung her head back, closing her eyes. Christ, she was beautiful. He'd fantasized about this moment and here she was, coming in all her glory in front of him.

Because of him.

He held her tight as she convulsed, her hips gyrating against his, her legs locked around his waist.

Her orgasm sent him flying over the edge, and he erupted inside her with a low growl. Scorching heat shot through his loins, and he swore he saw stars. He clutched her to him as he rode it out, absorbing every spasm of her body into his.

CHAPTER 26

*I*zzy clung to him until her body calmed down.

"Holy shit," she whispered. "That was—" Words failed her.

"Yeah." He slid out of her, gazing at her with something like awe.

She giggled, suddenly realizing she was naked. Where the hell had her bikini gone? He reached out and grasped it.

She gave an embarrassed laugh and took it from him. "Better put this on before I get out." The pool was still deserted, but anyone could come along at any moment.

Izzy climbed out of the pool, her body still tingling. She'd never experienced anything so wanton or so exciting before. Not with anyone.

Now, here was a man whose clothes she really did want to rip off. And had. Literally.

Viper Morgan was everything she'd fantasized about. And more. No way would she ever forget this.

Lying down on the lounge chair, she watched him as he ducked under the water, then pulled himself out of the pool, not using the steps. Water glistened off his muscular body, already tanned from the Mexican sun.

Viper wasn't traditionally good-looking like Phoenix, but he was rough and rugged and way sexier, in her opinion. She'd worked with enough tall, dark, and handsome model-types for their smooth, good looks to have lost their appeal.

No, thank you. She liked them a bit wild, a bit dangerous, a bit rough. And Viper was all those things.

The sun warmed her body, and as she basked in a post-coital haze, she didn't know when she'd ever felt so relaxed. Or aroused. The look in Viper's eyes made her feel like the sexiest girl on the planet.

He came over and sat down on the lounger beside her. "Careful you don't burn."

Was the sun shining? She hadn't noticed.

Actually, he was right. The rays were still intensely hot, and without protection, she'd burn.

Reaching over, she grabbed a bottle from her bag. "Would you mind?"

His eyes blazed into hers. "Sure."

She lay on her stomach while he rubbed the sunscreen on her back. His touch was gentle, but his hands were rough. She could feel the calluses and scar tissue. Even that was a turn-on. God, she was so hot for this guy.

He smoothed on the lotion, his hands fanning out over her shoulders and then down her sides to the small of her back. Heat radiated through her, and she barely managed not to squirm with excitement.

He squirted some more on her legs, the cold cream a stark contrast to the heat of the sun, or was it his hands? Long strokes, down her legs, then around her butt, to her inner thighs.

She moaned, unable to help it. God, she'd become this

wanton woman, on fire for him. His hand slowed. "I think that side is done."

His voice was throaty. Was he as turned on as she was?

She turned over and stared up at him. He poured lotion on his hands, rubbed them together, then massaged it into her stomach. Upwards and outwards, in big, lazy circles. She shivered as his fingertips brushed the underside of her breasts. Her nipples puckered, begging for his touch.

Still, he rubbed the lotion over her stomach, her sides, and then her chest and shoulders, studiously avoiding her breasts.

Sweet Jesus, she was melting here.

"Touch me," she whispered, arching toward him.

He knew what she meant. That electric blue gaze left her in no doubt about what he wanted to do to her. Sucking in a breath, he slid his hands under her bikini top and over her breasts. She sighed, closing her eyes. It felt exquisite. He caressed them, kneading them softly until her breath was fast and shallow.

She gasped as his thumbs grazed her nipples. A gentle squeeze and a spark ran through her body, culminating in a warmth that spread through her stomach and down to her loins. Her eyes flew open.

With his thumb and forefinger, he teased her nipples until they were bullet hard. Her chest heaved and her body trembled. Wetness pooled between her legs that had nothing to do with the dip she'd just taken. Only Viper could turn her into a quivering, shaking mess.

When she couldn't stand it anymore, he ran his hands down her stomach and then her thighs. She writhed under his touch, luxuriating in the sensations flooding her body. He knew just how to touch her to make her melt.

He slipped his fingers under her bikini bottom and ran

them over the soft, damp hair. Her pelvis rose toward him, eager and hungry for more.

A half-smile on his face, he moved his other hand back to her breast, where he carried on where he'd left off, while his fingertips parted her pussy lips and slid between her moist folds.

"Oh, shit," she gasped.

Sex in the pool had been impulsive and erotic, but this was an exquisite form of torture.

"Viper." She clutched his wrist.

His fingers delved deeper, and she parted her legs to give him better access. His aquamarine eyes held her captive as his thumb circled over her swollen nub.

"Oh…" she moaned, as the pressure built. His hand on her breast was sending shivers down to her core and his fingers were sending little shocks of pleasure upwards until she was a melting, writhing mess on the lounge chair.

Her breathing quickened as the lingering arousal from her past orgasm intensified. Desire built in waves, sending her higher and higher onto the crest. Her breath turned to moans and she heard herself mewing like a cat, but she couldn't seem to stop.

"Oh, yes…yes… yes!"

He kept the pressure on her clit, kept her rising until she couldn't get any higher.

"Oh my God!" She gripped his thigh as the wave came crashing down. At the same moment, a group of suited businessmen walked out onto the pool terrace.

Helpless, Izzy cried out, but Viper leaned forward and covered her mouth with his own, muffling the sound. His fingers didn't stop, but he shielded her body with his own, and she orgasmed beneath him, trembling like a leaf, as the waves crashed over her.

CHAPTER 27

*J*esus, she was beautiful. As he lay half on top of her, covering her body from prying eyes and feeling her come beneath him, a jolt of something he couldn't fathom spread through him. A protectiveness, a warmth mixed with desire and tenderness. It took his breath away.

She was so vulnerable in that moment, so completely his.

He kissed her gently as she came back down to earth.

The businessmen moved to the opposite side of the terrace, more concerned with their dealings than two people making out on a lounge chair.

Viper grabbed her sarong and covered her nakedness before sitting up.

Her cheeks were flushed, her eyes bright, and her wet hair snaked around her shoulders, the edges already drying in the hot sun. He'd seriously never seen anyone more beautiful in his entire life. "Are you okay?"

She smiled, still a little hazy. "More than okay."

She was positively glowing. He shifted uncomfortably, straining against his trunks. Making her come had worked him up again, and if he didn't cool down, he was going to erupt.

"I'm going to take a swim," he said, getting up. Within a few long strides, he dived back into the pool.

Thank fuck.

The water helped cool him down, but not as much as he'd hoped. At least it had reduced his erection to acceptable standards.

When he got out, Izzy was standing by the lounge chair, sarong wrapped around her body like a towel. Her eyes blazed with a deep intensity that made him catch his breath. In that moment, she was wild, wanton, and sexy as fuck.

She took his hand. "Let's go up to the room."

They didn't say much in the elevator, but she didn't let go of his hand. His heart thumped against his rib cage like it did before he jumped out of a helicopter into a war zone.

They walked down the corridor, and he opened their door. The moment they got inside, she pulled him into her arms.

"This is your fault," she murmured as the sarong fell to the floor. "You've made me so horny, I don't know what to do with myself."

He chuckled, releasing some of the tension. "You're not the only one."

What little good the pool water had done was quickly undone when she kissed him hard on the mouth. He picked her up, making her yelp, and carried her to the bed. He laid her down, conscious of her eyes on him, then peeled off his shorts and climbed on top of her.

She ripped off her sodden bikini and embraced him, naked and glorious. Her long legs wrapped around him like they had in the swimming pool, like he'd envisioned the first time they'd met. That unwanted thought that had shot into his mind during their first interview. Had it been a premonition?

Or just wishful thinking?

Either way, the reality was so much better.

He took her face in his hands and kissed her, claiming her mouth with his own. He wasn't going to hold back. She wanted him and fucking hell, he wanted her too. More badly than he'd wanted any woman in his entire life.

She clung to him like her life depended on it. He explored her mouth, ravaging it until they were both gasping for air, then her pelvis rose to meet him, and he slid inside her like it was the most natural thing in the world.

She cried out and bit down on his shoulder. He growled and grabbed fistfuls of her hair, anchoring himself on his elbows on either side of her head. She stared up at him, her eyes ablaze with hunger, desire, and need.

Jesus, this was crazy.

There was no time to think, as his body reacted to the beautiful woman beneath him. A primal force had taken over and there was no going back. He was too far gone.

He thrust into her velvety depths.

Christ, she felt good. She was so ready for him.

He dove into her, aware that he was very close to losing control.

"Faster," she moaned.

Shit, he *was* losing it.

He thrust manically, his head pounding, his whole body taut.

She felt so good, so tight, that he didn't think he could hold out much longer. The pressure built until he was groaning with the effort.

Then, she bucked beneath him, her legs tightening around his waist, her body turning rigid. He felt her clamp down on his swollen cock as her orgasm hit.

Fuuuck!

He exploded inside her, growling something incoherent as he came. He surged forward, thrusting into her as far as he could go. Fireworks went off in his brain and he closed his eyes, drowning in the release. Molten spasms shot through his body, hot and hard, over and over until he shuddered. Drained.

He relaxed his grip on her. She was still clinging to him like a barnacle. Feeling him relax, she let go and fell back onto the bed. Her breathing was labored, her hair disheveled and spread out all over the pillow. She looked like a goddess that had fallen from heaven.

He collapsed, half on top of her, their legs still intertwined. He put his head on the pillow next to her and tried to get his breathing under control.

Jesus. That was intense.

Neither of them spoke for a long moment. How did you put into words what had just happened? That had been so explosive, so unexpected, so unlike anything he'd ever experienced.

"Viper, I—" she whispered. A feeble attempt at something.

He looked at her and thought he saw tears, but she blinked them away.

"Yeah?"

Another long pause.

"Nothing." She touched his face and then climbed out of bed. "I need a shower. I'm covered in sunscreen."

He laughed. It eased this strange, unearthly tension that had enveloped them.

She flashed him a shaky smile, then padded to the bathroom, closing the door behind her.

*I*zzy stood in the shower, her head against the cool glass. She had yet to turn on the water.

What had just happened?

That was something else. It was out of this world insane. She'd never *ever* lost control like that before. Her lips throbbed from his hard kisses, her nipples tingled from his kneading, and her core pulsed with the lingering effects of her orgasm. Even now, she felt his hot seed trickling out of her.

It took several minutes of deep breathing before she could turn on the shower and climb under the cool water.

Viper.

Oh my god, Viper.

First in the pool, then on the lounge chair, and now in her hotel bed. Three orgasms in as many hours. And she still wanted more.

What was wrong with her?

Emily was right. With that man in her room, she might never leave.

He was sex on legs. A lethal hunk of a man with a

physique a Norse god would be proud of, eyes that simmered like the depths of the ocean, and an intensity that had ignited her soul. Burned through her defenses.

Hell, who was she kidding? She'd never had any defenses where he was concerned.

She soaped herself up and rubbed all the sticky sunscreen, sweat, and remnants of their lovemaking off her body. Once clean, she turned off the hot tap and blasted herself with cold. That would kill any lingering desire she had for him.

Gasping, she stood there as long as she could, then turned off the water.

There, she was back in control.

This was just a hookup. An insanely hot hookup, amplified by their situation and what they'd been through.

She'd been kidnapped, for Pete's sake. Who wouldn't want life-affirming sex with a man like Viper afterward?

Twice.

He was her protector, her bodyguard, the man who'd saved her life. That was so sexy. It was sheer adrenaline and gratitude that had made her behave so wildly. She mustn't read more into this than that.

Stepping out of the shower, she pulled on the soft toweling robe and fastened it around her waist. Then she stared into the blurry image in the mirror and combed her hair back off her face. There was a freedom in not wearing any makeup. She hadn't since they'd gotten here. Didn't have any anyway. All her belongings were back in D.C. Emily had probably arranged for them to be sent back to her apartment.

Or to Robert's.

Christ, Robert.

What would he say if he knew?

She turned away from the mirror. It was none of his business what happened between her and Viper. She wasn't engaged to him. They'd made no promises to each other. Of course, she knew that's what he wanted, but she wasn't sure. That's why she hadn't let their relationship progress past a few dates and a chaste kiss on the lips.

What was good for the company wasn't what was best for her. She needed more than what Robert could give her. More passion. More excitement. More everything.

More Viper.

She took a deep breath and came to a decision. They had a few days here at the most. A few days without anyone else around. Without cell phones. Without email. Without social media. Without meetings and budgets and orders.

If this was all she was going to get with Viper, she was sure as hell going to make it count, inhibitions be damned. After this, she'd go back to D.C. and he'd go back to... She realized she didn't even know where he lived.

Anyway, life would resume as normal. Her crazy, chaotic life that she loved, but that afforded her very little personal time. A life that he didn't fit into.

For these few days, it was going to be all about them. Decision made, she opened the door and went back into the room.

VIPER STOOD in the middle of the room, a worried expression on his face. "Everything okay?" He'd put his shorts back on for modesty's sake. She could tell he was anxious about what had happened. He'd been shaken by the intensity of their lovemaking too.

She kissed him boldly on the lips. "Yes, perfect."

His eyes widened in surprise. "Um, okay. You don't want to talk about what just happened?"

"No, why would I?"

He hesitated, then grinned. "Then I'll just go take a shower." And he disappeared into the steamy bathroom.

She put on a fresh dress, then sat on the bed and turned the television on to the CNN news channel. Home suddenly seemed very far away.

The reporter talked about the unseasonably hot weather and how the crowds were flocking to the country's beaches. How American Airlines had decided to strike right at the end of the vacation season, and how there was commuter chaos on the trains due to twisted railway tracks unable to stand the heat.

That's how I feel with Viper around, she thought, staring at the melted, buckled steel. Today being a case in point. Still, she did feel great. Why should she be ashamed of that? Wasn't she always telling her followers to love their bodies? To live life to the fullest?

Well, that's what she was doing. At least for the next few days.

This wouldn't last, it couldn't, but until then, he was all hers.

On cue, Viper stepped out of the bathroom, a towel wrapped around his waist. She let her gaze roam over his perfect torso, his washboard abs, his smattering of chest hair, and those wonderfully broad and reassuring shoulders that had enveloped her on so many occasions, keeping her safe.

He noticed her gaze and a smile tugged at his lips. "Anything interesting happening?"

She glanced back at the TV. "The east coast is having a heat wave," she said, blowing a strand of hair off her face.

"Oh, yeah?" He pulled on his shorts and was about to reach for a shirt when Izzy whispered, "Don't."

He let it go.

She flushed. "I like seeing your body."

He leaned over and kissed her on the lips. "You're the boss."

The picture on the television changed and Izzy found she was looking at a photograph of herself. "Oh, my gosh. Look!"

She turned up the volume.

"...*Isabelle Beaumont, who was abducted a week ago while on a yacht off the Californian coast has been found alive and well. Sources close to the social media entrepreneur and mining magnate say she's recovering with close friends and family and asks that the public respect her privacy at this difficult time.*"

"That's Emily's doing," she murmured.

"*Miss Beaumont was kidnapped while on investment banker, Casper Montague's yacht in San Diego. Eyewitnesses reported four armed gunmen boarded the vessel and took Miss Beaumont captive after a short, but violent gunfight. One man was injured in the attack. It is not clear why Miss Beaumont was targeted or how she was rescued, but there are rumors that her personal protection team was involved. The FBI, who are investigating Miss Beaumont's abduction, have refused to comment. We'll have more on this breaking news story as events unfold.*"

"You're a breaking news story." Viper sat down next to her on the bed.

"I don't mean to sound arrogant, but I'm used to being in the media." She turned to him with a rueful smile. "That doesn't faze me, but this will affect the share price. Robert's going to have his hands full pacifying the shareholders."

"I thought you owned the company?"

She leaned over and kissed his shoulder. "I own fifty-one percent of the company, the controlling share. That means nobody can buy me out, and I get to sign off on all the decisions."

"What about Robert?"

"He owns a portion, as does my cousin, Raf, but the rest is

owned by the public. It's a listed company and my disappearance would have shaken confidence."

Viper nodded. "What are you going to do?"

"Well, that press release Emily wrote will have helped. When I reappear, things will settle down."

When she reappeared. Her stomach clenched, and she shook her head. She didn't want to think about that now. They still had some time here. Even though she was well aware she was living in a blissful bubble, she didn't want it to burst. Not quite yet.

"Enough about that. I'm starving. Let's order room service."

He chuckled. "You'll get no argument from me there." They browsed the menu, then deciding what they were going to have, placed their order.

They were about to eat when the room phone rang. Izzy glanced at Viper in alarm. Nobody knew they were here other than Phoenix and Pat.

Viper answered. "Hello?"

She saw his shoulders relax. "It's Pat," he mouthed.

She nodded and turned down the television so he could talk, and she could overhear the conversation.

"Yeah, we're good. She's good. Hanging in there."

Izzy barely suppressed a grin.

"You want us to stay here for a few more days?" He nodded into the phone. "Sure, no problem."

Her heart leaped. They weren't being recalled. While she wanted this nightmare to be over, part of her didn't want to leave the resort and go back to reality. She wanted to keep things just as they were, at least for a few days longer. It looked like she'd get her wish.

"Will do. You can count on it."

He hung up and she raised an eyebrow. "Count on what?"

His blue eyes twinkled. "That I'll do my very best to look after you."

She laughed. "I'm sure that is not what Uncle Pat meant."

He snorted. "He's my boss. Hard to picture him as Uncle Pat."

Izzy was fond of the gruff former Commander. She'd always known he'd been a Navy SEAL, although that was a very long time ago now. "I've always known him as that. He's my godfather. He and my mother were close."

"How did they know each other?" He sat beside her on the bed.

She shrugged. "You know, I never did find out. When I was a girl, I remember barbecues at Pat and Val's house. I used to play in the backyard with their son, Joe."

"The one who died in Afghanistan?" Viper asked. He remembered Blade being particularly cut up about that.

She nodded sadly. "Yes, he was a good friend growing up, but then his mother got sick and died, and he joined the army. I think he was looking for something to replace her. Pat fell apart and my parents helped him out, or rather my mother did. My father was always down here, at the mines. She was a good friend to him. I think they knew each other from before, when Pat was starting out, but I could be wrong. Anyway, he was always at our house."

Viper pursed his lips.

Izzy shook her head. "I know what you're thinking, but you're wrong. I saw how devastated Pat was when Val died. He and my mother were just old friends. That's all there was to it."

"And then he lost his son."

She nodded. "That was tough. He was so proud of Joe. I lost touch with him when he joined the army, but he had a girlfriend by then. Lily, her name was. They met in high school and were inseparable. Still, it was a shock when he passed."

"It always is." He fell silent and she realized he must have lost friends and colleagues in his profession too. She took his hand and gave it a squeeze.

Room service arrived, and they sat around the small table, eating and talking. Izzy had ordered a bottle of wine, so she poured them each a glass. "My mother loved a glass of chilled Sauvignon Blanc in the evening," she said, wistfully.

"What happened to your mother?" Viper asked, softly.

"She died in a car accident on Christmas Eve six years ago."

"A car accident? Like your father?"

"Ironic, isn't it? Although, her death had nothing to do with his. Dad was home for the holidays, but he'd been away a lot, and they'd had a row. I heard them yelling at each other from my bedroom. It was awful. My mother stormed out of the house. It was a freezing cold winter, and the roads were icy. She was going too fast and skidded out of control. She smashed into a tree and died instantly."

He put down his burger and stared at her. "Shit, that's awful. I'm sorry."

Izzy took a deep breath, letting the painful memories flow over her. She'd learned a long time ago not to bottle things up. *Let it go,* the grief counselor had said. *Don't be afraid to feel.*

Words she'd taken to heart.

Exhaling, she said, "For a long time, I blamed my father for her death. Of course, he didn't stick around long. As soon as we'd buried her, he was back here, doing what he does."

Viper shook his head. "Doesn't sound like he was a very hands-on dad."

"He wasn't. Pat was always there for me, though. He helped me through it."

"Pat's a good man," Viper said. "Or so I hear. I don't really know him that well, to be honest. Only by reputation."

"It's all true. He's been very good to me over the years."

"So when did you start up your business?" Viper asked, before picking up his burger and taking a massive bite.

"Shortly after my mother's death. Up until then, I'd been in the papers a lot, mostly because I was Astrid Beaumont's daughter. My mother was a famous Brazilian supermodel. People wondered if I'd follow in her footsteps, but that life wasn't for me."

Viper's eyebrows rose. "A model?"

"Yeah, can you believe it? Still, I had quite a following on social media, so I decided to put it to good use. I negotiated a few contracts with some fashion houses and became something of a brand ambassador. My following grew and it went from there. Now I try to help women look good no matter what their size or budget."

"You've done extremely well." The way he was looking at her. Pride mixed with something else. Something she didn't want to put a name to.

"I like what I do. That helps. It doesn't feel like work."

"Do you miss it? Being here, unable to work?" His blue eyes flickered, but only momentarily.

"Viper?"

"Yeah?"

"I like having you here to myself. Let's enjoy these next few days, before we have to go back to reality."

"If you're sure," he said, his deepening blue gaze on her face as if he were trying to read her.

She reached across the table and took his hand. "Oh, I'm sure."

CHAPTER 29

*V*iper didn't know when he'd ever been this happy.

Sure, he'd had successful ops that had made him happy, ecstatic even. Flings that were memorable, but they all paled in comparison to the heady, intoxicating few days with Izzy.

They'd spent *a lot* of time in their room making love. She'd surprised him with her spontaneity. When she let down her guard and opened up, she was funny and entertaining, even a little wild. He loved that about her.

Then there was the way she'd just let go and embraced their time together. Viper felt privileged that he'd caught a rare glimpse of the *real* Izzy Beaumont, the part that nobody else saw. The part she kept hidden under her professional demeanor and her carefully curated social profile. This side of her, only her best friends and a few lucky lovers got to see.

They'd swum in the hotel pool and gone for long walks on the beach. They'd talked about their pasts and their childhoods, and he'd told her things he'd never told anyone, not even his buddies in the military.

"Don't you remember your parents at all?" she asked one

afternoon after they'd skinny-dipped in the ocean and were drying off on a big towel before walking back to the hotel.

"Not really. After my mother died, I was sent to live with my grandparents, and when they died, I was put into foster care. My only memory is a hazy woman with dark hair singing me a lullaby, but that could also be something I dreamed up along the way."

She'd looked at him with such tenderness. "I'm sorry you had such a hard start in life."

He shrugged. "It wasn't that bad. I was fifteen when my grandfather died, and sixteen when I enlisted. So, I was only in foster care for ten months, and I spent most of it camping in the woods behind my new family's house." He grinned at her. "It made me a lot more resilient during SEAL training. I was used to living off the land, fending for myself."

Her eyes had welled with sympathy. "No child should have to live like that."

"I was a big fifteen-year-old. I could look after myself."

"I'm sure you could." She ran her hands down his arms, her fingertips tracing his biceps, triceps, and forearms. "But it's still not right."

"No, but that's life, right? We just have to make the best of whatever situation we find ourselves in."

"Can't argue with you there." And she'd wriggled on top of him and kissed him until his head spun. They'd made love on the beach before walking back, hand in hand.

Was this what a real relationship was like?

He had nothing to base it on. His past relationships had been short-lived flings and one-night stands with women he knew from the local bar. With his schedule, he never knew when he'd be called up for an op or deployed into a war zone. Consequently, he'd never looked for anyone that he couldn't say goodbye to and not look back.

Until now.

But he wasn't a goddamned fool. He knew this perfect idyll wouldn't last.

Izzy had to get back to work and he had to get back to guarding her. The question he was afraid to ask was: where did that leave their relationship?

Maybe it was best not to dwell on it.

Live in the moment. Wasn't that what Izzy was doing?

He was used to living like that. During a mission, you had no choice but to live in the moment. When bullets were flying by and grenades were exploding around you, all you could think about was survival. Nothing else mattered. Any peripheral thought, any distraction could get you killed.

That's why he made sure he never had any.

He realized his mistake in letting his guard down when they were walking back into the hotel after a stroll around the moonlit gardens and a man in khaki combat pants and a black shirt stepped out of the bushes.

Viper saw him first, and shoved Izzy behind him. She gasped, as he drew his weapon. He'd stopped wearing his vest, but he never went anywhere without his Glock.

"Don't be alarmed," said the stranger. "I only want to talk."

"Who are you?" Viper leveled his pistol at the intruder.

"My name is Gert Henderson, CEO of GHMG Holdings."

"The mining conglomerate?" Izzy said, poking her head out from behind him.

"Yes, Miss Beaumont. If you wouldn't mind, I'd like a few minutes of your time."

He was overly polite and spoke with a slight accent. German, maybe.

"Do you have any identification?" Viper didn't like this. He didn't care who this guy was, but you don't just appear out of nowhere asking to talk. That's not how it worked. And how the hell did he know who Izzy was, anyway?

More importantly, how'd he know she was here?

"Sure." The man reached into his back pocket.

"Slowly," hissed Viper. Izzy had her hand on his back. He could hear her short, shallow breaths. His only thought was to keep her from harm.

The stranger handed over a German passport. Viper didn't drop his gun. "You take it," he said to Izzy.

She reached around him and glanced at the photograph. "It's him," she whispered. "Gert Henderson."

"Are you alone?" Viper asked. He hadn't picked up any other movement, but that didn't mean they weren't there.

"Of course not," he said honestly. "This is Mexico and I'm not crazy. My yacht is anchored off the coast. We sailed up from Costa Rica to talk to Miss Beaumont."

"How did you know she was here?" Viper was seriously worried. They could be surrounded. Outgunned again. He knew one thing thought, they were taking Izzy over his dead body.

"I have my sources."

"Nobody knew we were here," whispered Izzy. There was fear in her voice.

"Shall we go and sit down and then I'll tell you how I found you," said the man.

Viper nodded. There'd be more people on the terrace. Less chance of a firefight. "After you."

They followed the stranger onto the pool terrace and sat down at one of the tables. The umbrellas had been taken down for the night and the stars twinkled unknowingly overhead.

Viper aimed his gun under the table. "Any suspicious moves and you risk losing a vital part of your anatomy."

The man nodded and put his hands on the table. "I told you, I'm here to talk."

"Why couldn't this have waited until I got back to D.C.?" Izzy asked.

"Because this is off the books, so to speak. I don't want my shareholders to know what we're discussing and I sure as hell don't want yours to either."

Viper frowned. Perhaps this wasn't a kidnap attempt, but he wasn't ready to rule anything out. "Where are your men?"

"On the beach. They're not a threat."

He felt some of the tension drain from his shoulders. "Okay, talk. How did you find us?"

"It wasn't that hard. I managed to get hold of your boyfriend's call records and traced the incoming call from this hotel two days after you were abducted. Robert Hampton-Barnes."

Izzy sat up straight. "Firstly, Robert isn't my boyfriend, and how did you get his call records? Isn't that illegal?"

"Like I said, I have my sources. I knew you'd been kidnapped in San Diego and figured you'd be holed up here somewhere until the heat died down."

Shit. If this guy had found them, the cartel could too.

Izzy slumped back in her chair. "I should report you to the authorities."

He shrugged. "Why don't you wait until you hear what I have to say?"

She sighed. "Okay, fine. Go ahead."

Viper kept the gun angled at the man's genitals. One false move and his balls were going to get blown to bits.

"As you know, my company owns many mines in Central America. We mostly operate gold mines, but iron ore accounts for 5% of our portfolio."

Could he have hired the mercs who'd kidnapped Izzy?

Izzy was listening, her arms folded in front of her. She might be in a strappy sundress, her hair wild and free down her back, but her face was all business.

"What do you want with me?"

"I'd like to make you an offer. We've done surveys in

Mexico, and we've found a high likelihood of rutile and bauxite in the mountains of Montezuma. We'd like to extend the mine's capabilities into these base metals as well. As you know, rutile is used in the manufacture of..."

"Titanium," she cut in. "And bauxite in aluminum."

"Correct." He smiled at her. "You know your metals, Miss Beaumont."

She certainly did. And she was as cool as a cucumber. Viper felt a surge of pride, then swallowed it down and focused on the threat.

She was staring at the Henderson, frowning. "You want to buy me out?"

"Yes, to put it plainly. We have an excellent record in Central America. We employ workers from the local communities, we provide infrastructure and amenities, we respect the environment. We're not some power-hungry conglomerate that drills holes in the ground and leaves destruction in our wake."

"That's all very impressive, Mr. Henderson. I'm aware of your company's work ethic. It's one of your strongest selling points. But what makes you think I want to sell my share of Omega Enterprises?"

He smiled. "Come on, Miss Beaumont. We both know this isn't your game. Your father ran the company for twenty years, building it from the ground up. He ventured where no other company was willing to go. The risk was high, yet somehow, he made it work. Now others are following in his footsteps. The region has an abundance of raw materials, mostly squandered by corrupt officials and unscrupulous conglomerates. By rights, it should be one of the richest continents in the world, instead it's the poorest."

He had a point there.

Izzy listened to all this, her head tilted to the side.

"You're a businesswoman in your own right. Fashion is

your thing. Not minerals. That's why you made Robert Hampton-Barnes CEO, a man who doesn't even have a controlling share of the company. Why don't you hand it over to someone whose interests align with yours?"

"How do you know what my interests are?" she said.

"I know you won't release your share of the company because you're worried about the communities the mine supports. I know you've refused offers from several conglomerates looking to expand into the area. I know the situation in Mexico is volatile and you're concerned that if you sell the mine, it will cause more instability. I know you're worried about your employees losing their jobs."

"How do you know all this?" she breathed.

Viper stiffened beside her. Good question. One he'd like to know too.

"I've been studying you, Miss Beaumont. From afar, of course. Don't worry, it's nothing nefarious. I'm not a stalker. My interest is purely business. I can see you're a good person, but that your interests lie elsewhere."

"So you thought you'd take the company off my hands, is that right? Do me a favor?"

"Exactly." He sat back and smiled at her. A long moment passed, after which he said, "I wanted to have this chat face to face, because after the attempt on your life, I thought you might be anxious to sell your stake."

Viper scowled. "That was your doing?"

His hand tightened on the gun.

Henderson put his hands in the air. "No, absolutely not. I must say, I'm very pleased you're all right. I take it this is your savior?" He nodded at Viper.

Izzy didn't reply.

"Why didn't you pick up the phone and call me? Why now? Here?"

Another excellent question.

"Because this is a frank conversation, Miss Beaumont. I'm being honest with you. I want the best for those communities too. I wanted to reassure you that my company will uphold what your father has created and go even further. It's hard to explain that in a boardroom filled with overzealous negotiators."

He had a point.

Viper looked at Izzy. She was pursing her lips like she did when she was contemplating something.

"Mr. Henderson, I don't know what you thought you'd achieve by ambushing me like this, but I've heard what you had to say. Now I'd appreciate it if you left."

He stood up. So did Viper.

"I understand. Sorry to intrude on your... vacation." His gaze shifted to the gun in Viper's hand. "But you understand why I wanted to talk to you before you got back to D.C.? Your CEO would shut me down before I even got going."

"He'd be justified in doing so. He'd lose everything if I sold out," she said, defensively.

Henderson merely shrugged.

Izzy got to her feet. "I think you should go now."

He followed suit. "Will you at least think about it?"

"I will, but I'm not making any promises."

"Fair enough." Henderson nodded at Viper before walking away.

Viper watched him go. It was only when Henderson had disappeared in the direction of the beach that he let his hand drop.

CHAPTER 30

"I can't believe that guy," Izzy said, once he'd gone. The meeting had shaken her more than she cared to admit. "Surprising us like that."

Viper holstered his gun. "The worrying thing is how he found us. If he can, so can the bad guys. We're not safe here anymore."

She sighed. "You're right. I suppose it's time to head back to D.C. I can't stay away much longer anyway, my followers will be getting antsy. Besides, I have to meet with the board members about the mine. They don't even know that my father was murdered."

It was all rushing back. The responsibility, the threats, the fear.

"Did you believe him?" asked Viper as they walked back inside. "Henderson, I mean."

"Yeah, I did. I've heard my father talk about GHMG Holdings before. He was praising their work in Nicaragua. If I was going to sell to anyone—" She frowned. "I just don't like being ambushed."

"Can't argue with you there." Viper checked the corridor as the elevator opened.

Izzy sighed. "So, we're back to looking over our shoulders everywhere we go?"

"Unfortunately, yeah. We've become careless these last few days. *I've* become careless. I should have kept my guard up."

She took his hand. "I thought we were safe here too."

They went into their room. The window was open, letting in the warm breeze. After being so relaxed these last few days, the tension was back. She stretched her neck and tried to push it away. "Okay if we fly back tomorrow?"

He nodded. "I'll clear it with Pat, but it's probably for the best. I don't know how much longer we'll be safe here, now that our location has been compromised."

"Henderson won't tell anyone."

"You can't be sure of that. Anyway, anyone tracing Robert or Emily's phone will know."

Izzy sat down on the bed. The last few days had been like a dream. She couldn't believe they're coming to an end.

Sensing her mood, Viper sat down beside her. "We still have tonight."

She turned and threw her arms around his neck. He smelled so good, felt so good, that she wanted to hang on forever. "I know, and I intend to make the most of it."

MUCH LATER, as Izzy lay in a post-orgasmic haze, she thought about Henderson's offer. What would Robert and Raf say if she sold her share to GHMG? They'd object, for sure. Henderson would bring in his own team to run things, absorb their company into his own.

Except, nobody knew the company like Robert, and Raf to a lesser extent. And what about all the other people who worked for Omega Enterprises? Would their jobs, their livelihoods be on the line too? Every decision she made affected so many other people.

To be honest, it would be a relief to offload the company and go back to concentrating on her own enterprise, but what were the consequences? Her father had left her with a responsibility that she couldn't take lightly.

She turned to Viper, sleeping silently beside her. At least, she thought he was asleep. His breathing was even and steady, but she was never sure with him. He woke up at the slightest noise. Instantly alert, like he'd been awake the entire time. Another occupational hazard, she guessed. Even when he was sleeping, it felt like he was watching over her.

She'd miss having him beside her.

Not as a bodyguard, but as a partner.

These past few days...

She smiled as she thought about what they'd done, how they'd been with each other. It had been perfect. Apart from the way they'd gotten here, she wouldn't change a thing.

THEIR FLIGHT LANDED at Dulles International Airport at three o'clock that afternoon. They'd caught a taxi to Mexico City earlier that morning and flown first-class back to D.C. Izzy had been on edge the entire time.

She had to resist the urge to take his hand. Now that they were home, she had to keep up pretenses. She pushed aside the heaviness in her heart and took a steadying breath. This was her reality now, and they both had to deal with it.

"You okay?" Viper glanced down at her.

She nodded and forced a smile. He looked ridiculous walking through the airport in his shorts, dolphin T-shirt, and leather sandals, especially with his imposing bulk and height. She noticed how people eyed him up, then moved out of the way as they came through. Thankfully, it was the end of August, American in the midst of a heatwave, and people were returning from summer vacations with bronzed faces and mismatched tan lines. In that respect, they fit right in.

Pat had sent a car for them. A woman in a pantsuit with flaming red hair stood at Arrivals holding a sign that read "Victoria Granger".

Izzy smiled. Viper must have told them the name she'd checked in under.

"That's me," she said, coming to a stop. They had very little baggage, just canvas bags containing the few things they'd bought from the hotel store.

The woman nodded and held out a hand. "Rose Clayton, but everyone calls me Thorn. I work for Blackthorn Security."

"Izzy Beaumont," Izzy said, shaking it. "Why Thorn?"

"I'm prickly, I guess." She grinned.

"Viper Morgan."

"It's good to meet you, Viper," Thorn said, nodding at him with respect. "I heard about what you did in Colombia. Great job."

Izzy turned to look at him. That's where he'd been shot.

"It was nothing."

Thorn punched him on the arm. "Don't be modest, Viper." She turned to Izzy. "This guy saved a whole bunch of people in a resort shooting a couple of months back. He's a hero."

She could have sworn Viper was blushing. "I didn't do anything anyone else wouldn't have done."

Thorn scoffed. "You went into a resort under attack and saved lives when most people were running in the opposite direction."

Izzy gazed at him in wonder. Why didn't that surprise her? He'd come for her, after all. She could just imagine him springing into action over a terrorist attack.

He was a hero. Not just her hero, but other people's too.

He strode ahead, eyes on the ground.

"I didn't know," she murmured to Thorn. She'd read about it, of course. The resort attack had been on the news channels and in the papers, but she hadn't known Viper was the mysterious special forces operative who'd gone in and gotten people out.

"Are the FBI any closer to proving the cartel wrote those letters?" Viper asked, changing the subject.

"I'll let Pat brief you on that," Thorn said. "I'm not a hundred percent on the details. It's not my case."

He gave a curt nod.

They got into the car. Thorn opened the back door for Izzy. She glanced at Viper to see if he'd sit beside her, but he walked around to the passenger door. It was protocol and they had to keep up appearances.

Thorn was a confident driver. She navigated the junctions and intersections as they left the airport with ease, and then joined the flow of traffic back to D.C. "So, you two have had quite an adventure," Thorn said, once they were in the fast lane, overtaking the slower cars on the interstate.

"You could say that." Izzy glanced at the back of Viper's head, slowly moving from left to right and back again, constantly alert. "I owe my life to Viper and Phoenix."

"Pat is so glad you're safe," she said. "He's waiting for you at HQ."

"Is that where we're going?" Izzy asked.

"Yeah. I know you're probably desperate to get home, but it won't take long. He wants to debrief you and give you an update on the investigation."

She sighed inwardly. All she wanted to do was take a shower, get changed into her own clothes, and fall into bed. Preferably with Viper, but she knew that was not going to happen. Not anymore. Not now they were back. He was her bodyguard, and she was the client, or principal, as he called it. Their closeness at the resort seemed to be fading away, and there was nothing she could do about it. "Okay."

"I HOPE you don't mind if Blade joins us," Pat said. They were sitting in his office, on the comfy chairs, around a small coffee table, two cups of coffee in front of them. Viper was close enough to touch, but he was stoically refusing to look at her.

"Not at all." Izzy had only met Blade briefly. He was a giant of a man, at least a head taller than everyone else, and broader than most. While his stature was intimidating, he had a reassuring smile, and exuded the same kind of masculine capability that Viper did.

As he came in and perched on the edge of Pat's desk, she wondered how he found clothes to fit him. He really was enormous.

"Excellent job in getting her back," Blade said, shaking Viper's hand.

"Thanks, but I had help."

"I heard."

"Izzy, when you're ready." Pat nodded at her to proceed.

She took a deep breath and thought back to the party on the yacht. "I was talking to Robert on the deck of Casper's sailboat, when all of a sudden, four masked men jumped over the side and grabbed me. They threw me into a small motorboat and took me to this old fishing trawler that was moored some distance away."

"We know that much," said Blade. "Viper followed you on the jet ski. That's how we knew the name of the ship."

"You followed me?" He'd neglected to mention that part.

"Only as far as I could," he muttered. "Then I ran out of gas."

"The Coast Guard picked him up some time later," Blade supplied. "Luckily they found him, otherwise he'd have been drifting for days."

Viper ground his jaw. "There were a lot of vessels in that vicinity. Someone would have spotted me eventually."

Izzy stared at him. The guy wasn't afraid of anything.

She carried on with her story. "They hauled me onboard and locked me up in this stinking cabin."

"Did you see their faces?" asked Pat.

She shook her head.

"I did," Viper cut in, and proceeded to tell them about the golfers at the hotel in San Diego, how they'd chatted up Emily, and how he and Phoenix had cut them down in the jungle in Mexico.

Izzy sat quietly, taking it all in. The terror she'd felt on that trawler, the fear in the jungle, it would never leave her. Viper had killed for her. What guy did that?

"The FBI pulled some prints from their hotel room," Pat said. "They can match them against the bodies in the jungle. Do you know where you landed?"

"I could probably work it out," Viper said.

Pat nodded. "They'll send a team down to retrieve them."

"I just want it to be over," Izzy whispered.

Pat leaned over and took her hand. "We'll get the people who kidnapped you, Izzy. Don't worry about that. It's just a matter of time."

She saw Viper nod in agreement. Why didn't she feel as confident?

"Unless they come for me again, we've got nothing. The FBI might be able to identify the mercenaries, but how will they prove the cartel is behind this?"

The men didn't have an answer.

She took a deep breath. "We could use me as bait."

"No."

"No way!"

"Absolutely not."

All three men spoke at the same time.

"Hear me out. If we set up the perfect kidnapping opportunity, then you guys could swoop in and catch them, and this nightmare will be over once and for all."

"I'm not prepared to put you at risk," said Pat firmly.

"They might not resort to kidnapping again," added Viper. He didn't need to explain. He meant this time they might just kill her. Easier. Quicker. Cleaner.

No more bargaining.

She swallowed. "They won't. I'm useless to them dead, remember. Raf will inherit my share of the company and the status quo will remain unchanged. They need us to sell, which means they have to use me as leverage."

"Let's table that for later." Pat glanced at Blade worriedly. "In the meantime, we'll keep working on it. Viper will continue to be your personal protection agent."

She nodded, her gaze shifting to her lover, the man who'd shared her every moment for the last week, give or take. He still wouldn't look directly at her. Maybe he was afraid his boss would realize that they'd been sleeping together and fire him.

"Unless you'd rather I assigned someone else?"

"I'm okay with it," Viper blurted out, at the same time as she said, "That's okay. I trust Viper. I don't want anyone else guarding me."

Pat nodded. "Okay, good. We'll be in touch. Take care, Izzy, and call if you see anything suspicious."

She stood up and hugged him. "I will. Thanks, Uncle Pat. I appreciate all you're doing."

He smiled. "You're in good hands."

She snuck a look at Viper behind Pat's back. "I know."

CHAPTER 31

The sun was beginning to sink below the skyline when Thorn dropped them off outside Izzy's apartment block. Viper stared up at the elegant four-storey building with wide, expansive balconies overlooking the quiet crescent-shaped street. Very nice.

"Thanks, Thorn." He climbed out, then walked around and opened the car door for Izzy.

"See you soon," the operative called before driving off.

The concierge hurried out to meet them. "Welcome back, Miss Beaumont." He smiled fondly at her. "I was glad to read you were okay after your ordeal."

"Thank you, Lewis." She gave him a tired smile. "I'm just glad to be home."

"Your luggage arrived from San Diego a few days ago," Lewis told her. "I've put it in your apartment."

"Thank you." She touched his arm, then walked inside.

Viper lingered behind to speak to him. "Do you have spare keys to all the apartments?"

"Yes, of course."

Viper lowered his voice. "Due to the continuing threat to

Miss Beaumont's life, it's imperative that nobody gains access to her apartment."

"I understand, sir," he said earnestly. "I'd never give the key to anyone."

Viper looked him over. Middle-aged, with thinning hair, but upright and light-footed, the concierge looked like he could handle himself.

"Even if they had a gun to your head?" he asked.

The concierge swallowed. "Should I give you the spare key to Miss Beaumont's apartment?"

"I think that would be wise. Thank you, Lewis."

As they walked past reception, he darted into the office and opened a steel cabinet by punching in a code. Viper watched him through the glass panel in the door. At least it was secure.

"Here you are." He handed the key to Viper, who put it straight into his pocket.

"Thanks. I'll see it's returned to you when I leave. Is this the only spare?"

A nod. "Yes, sir."

"Was that necessary?" asked Izzy as they took the elevator to the top floor. Of course, she'd have the penthouse.

"It's safer for him too," Viper explained. "If he's under duress, he won't be able to give them the key. He can open the cabinet and prove it's not there."

She gave a little nod. "I suppose so. But let's face it, if those armed men come bursting in here, Lewis isn't going to be much of a defense."

He gave a grim smile. "That's why you've got me."

She raised her eyebrows, then opened the door to her apartment. "I'm so tired, all I want is a soak in the tub and to go to bed."

Viper followed her in. He felt well-rested after the flight, and the debrief hadn't bothered him, even though it had been fairly long. The hardest part was ignoring her, so that his boss wouldn't guess they'd slept together. Pat had a soft spot where Izzy was concerned, and he didn't want to get him pissed. He couldn't afford to lose this job. The glimpse he'd had at what life was like without it had scared him. Scared him more than being alone.

"Izzy, we need to talk about what happened," he said reluctantly.

She sighed, her shoulders sinking. "I know."

He dumped his bag on the floor and took her hands in his. "I don't want this to end, but I don't see how we can keep seeing each other under these circumstances. Not without everybody finding out."

"We can't," she whispered, taking a step back. He let her go. Fuck, this was hard. Harder than he thought it would be. His gut wrenched at the thought of not holding her in his arms anymore, not laughing with her, or watching her eyes light up when he kissed her.

He watched as she turned and flopped onto the sofa. "So, we're going to call it quits? It's over?"

"Yeah. It's over." She looked up at him. "We always knew it was a temporary thing. A beautiful, brief affair while we were away. The circumstances were unique in Mexico. It was just the two of us. It's different now. You have your job to do, I have mine."

Protecting her. Making sure she was safe.

While she went shopping, organized photoshoots, built her online media empire. Then there were the mines, the shareholders, the business.

Their two worlds were so different. He knew she was right, so why did it hurt so goddamn much?

"Okay." He exhaled, ignoring the nausea that threatened to rise in his throat. "I wish it could be different, but your uncle…" He didn't need to continue.

She gave a dry chuckle. "Yeah, Pat would skin you alive."

He cringed. That wasn't the worst of it. He could not afford to lose this job.

Izzy pursed her lips. "You're not going to start calling me ma'am again, are you?"

He gave a sad smile. "Not unless you want me to."

"I think we're way past that."

He remembered gasping her name only last night, as he came inside her, right after she'd screamed his. They'd held each other for a long time, way into the early hours, each trying to make the moment last as long as possible.

"For what it's worth, I had a great time," he told her.

Her eyes gleamed softly, and for a moment the Izzy he knew intimately was back. "So did I."

Viper let her get settled and checked out the security in her apartment. The windows were all double-glazed and soundproof. You could fire a gun in here and it wouldn't be heard outside the apartment. He was almost done when a telephone rang.

"That's my landline," she muttered before answering it. She paused, listened, and then said, "Hello, Robert."

Viper stood still. What did that idiot want now? He pretended to inspect the lock on the balcony door as he listened.

"I'm exhausted. Can't it wait until tomorrow?"

It was a high-grade quality security locking mechanism. Not unbreachable if you knew what you were doing but would stump most common burglars.

He felt Izzy's eyes on him. "Okay, see you then."

She hung up.

Viper turned and raised an eyebrow.

"I have to go into the office first thing tomorrow morning," she said. "Jackson Ferris, who runs the mine in Mexico, is in D.C. Robert wants him to brief the board on the latest attack on Montezuma."

He could tell by the determined jut of her chin that this wasn't debatable. She'd get no argument from him. The sooner they got back to her normal routine, the better.

"What time do you want to leave?"

"Around nine o'clock."

He nodded. "I'll be here."

She hesitated. "You're not staying over?"

"I don't think that's part of the job."

"I didn't mean *with* me. I just meant here." He could tell she didn't want to be alone, but how would he explain to his boss that he'd stayed over? No one would believe it was in the spare room. It would be as damning as if he'd been in her bed.

"I can't, Izzy. I'm sorry."

She bit her lip. "I understand."

"I'll see you tomorrow. Call me if you need anything?"

But she'd turned and walked into the bathroom, leaving him to see himself out.

CHAPTER 32

Viper followed Izzy into the towering skyscraper that housed the D.C. offices for Omega Enterprises. The company took up the top five floors. In the reception area, he saw a board listing departments like Internal Audit, Facilities Engineering, Functional Materials, Environmental & Safety, Resource Development, and an entire floor for human resources, administration, accounting, finance, planning, and public relations.

The size of the organization hit him hard. *This* was what Izzy was in charge of? Holy shit.

He could barely handle his own life, let alone run a multi-billion-dollar corporation. She was in an entirely different league. What a fool he'd been to think they could ever make it work.

"We're on the 24th floor," she said as the elevator took them up.

They stepped out into a marble-floored lobby with soft lighting and a huge print by some famous artist on the wall. Glass sliding doors hissed open as they approached, leading them into a carpeted hallway.

"The boardroom is this way," Izzy said, marching ahead.

She pushed open a walnut-colored door and disappeared inside. Viper followed, his senses on high alert. The risk here was minimal, but he was ready for anything. He'd been caught off guard before. He had his Kevlar vest on under his shirt and jacket, and his pistol holstered at the small of his back.

Izzy looked incredible in a long dark-blue denim skirt with a slit up the side showing off her long legs, and a pressed, white shirt. She had on blood-red pumps with two-inch heels.

Viper watched as she greeted the people around the table. At the head was Robert, who, annoyingly, hugged her like a lost love, kissing her on both cheeks and holding her hand for way too long.

He glared at him as he took up his position at the door.

"Raf, how lovely to see you." Izzy embraced a younger man with dark brown hair and a harsh, angular face. He was good-looking in a debonair sort of way. Average height, slender build, expensive suit. Probably had manicured fingernails.

"Darling, I'm so glad you made it back in one piece. We were crazy with worry."

Viper doubted that. Rafael seemed far too self-absorbed to care about anyone else other than himself. Still, Viper didn't know the man, so he shouldn't judge.

Also in the room were four other men in designer suits with important expressions. They all shook Izzy's hand. He watched their faces closely, looking for any resentment or animosity but saw none.

"Jackson, it's good to see you again." Izzy shook hands with a stocky, blond man in an ill-fitting suit. The manager of Montezuma. This guy was more comfortable in his khakis, it was obvious. Big, brawny with scarred worker's hands and short fingernails. Viper liked him immediately.

"Miss Beaumont, I sure am glad you're okay." He was American, but with a definite Texan twang.

"Thank you. Shall we get down to business? I know you have a lot to tell us about what's happening at Montezuma."

"Yes, ma'am."

They sat down. Viper noticed there were two silver urns on the table containing tea and coffee and an assortment of cookies. There were also several pitchers of water. Izzy poured herself a glass of water.

"What is the situation in Mexico at the moment?" asked Robert, getting them going.

Jackson put his hands on the table. "The region is controlled by La Sombra Roja. The people are too scared to stand up to them, even the police are on their payroll. They own everyone."

"And they want the mine?" asked Izzy.

"Yes, ma'am. They don't want us there. We bring stability to the region, which makes them less powerful. We bring jobs and infrastructure, which makes the local communities less dependent on them."

Viper could understand that. Gangsters of any kind loved instability. It was how they operated.

"The mining rights were sold to us by the Mexican government," said Robert. "We have permission to mine that land. They have no right to it."

"They're responsible for these attacks?" Izzy asked.

Jackson nodded. "We managed to foil another attack a few days ago. Our security operatives apprehended two of the assailants, who we've handed over to the Mexican police."

"Good," said Robert. "Hopefully it will deter future attacks."

The FBI would be curious to know about that. He made a mental note to tell Pat.

"We hope so," agreed Jackson, although his gaze said he knew otherwise. They talked about the mine for a while longer, ironing out some operational issues, and finally Jackson got up and left. Viper followed him into the hall.

"We need to discuss the offers on the table for the company," Izzy was saying.

"Excuse me, Mr. Ferris." Viper closed the door behind him.

The man turned around, surprised at being approached by a member of security. "Yes?"

"I'm Viper Morgan, Miss Beaumont's personal protection officer. Do you mind if I ask you some questions?"

He hesitated, but only for a moment. "I guess so."

They walked toward the marble lobby. "Do you think the cartel could have hired someone to kill Richard Beaumont?"

The manager hesitated. "It's possible. His death was suspicious. Richard drove that road every day. I was surprised to hear he'd gone off the cliff like that."

"These two men the police have in custody—"

"As far as I know, they haven't admitted to anything. Like I said, the local police are corrupt, and will probably let them go."

More important than ever to get the FBI down there ASAP.

"Okay, thanks. If you hear of anything, will you let us know?" He handed the man one of the business cards that he'd gotten off Pat during their debrief. "That's my boss. You can reach me through him."

Jackson left, and Viper went back to the boardroom. He stood outside the door, not wanting to interrupt, and waited until the board meeting was finished. An hour later, the door opened, and everybody filed out.

"Let's go." Izzy walked past him. She seemed to be in a hurry.

"Izzy, wait up!" Robert caught up, ignoring Viper who hung back. "Can we talk?"

"What about?" She turned to face him.

His voice dropped. "About us. You and me."

She sighed. "Robert, there is no us. I'm sorry, but I just don't see you in that way. You're my friend and business partner, that's all there is to it."

His face hardened and Viper didn't like the look in his eye. "I'd still like to talk. We haven't had a chance to catch up since you got back and there are things we need to discuss. What you said about potentially selling the company, for example. I think we should discuss it."

"I can't tonight, Robert. I've got plans."

"With him?" Robert shot an angry glance in Viper's direction.

"No, Robert. He's my bodyguard." She sighed impatiently. "I've got to go."

Robert didn't give up. "I'm sorry. That was uncalled for. The kidnapping, getting shot, it's all been a strain. Let's go somewhere quiet and talk. How about tomorrow night?"

Her gaze flickered to Viper, then back to Robert. "Okay, fine."

"Great, I'll pick you up at eight."

Viper kept quiet as they took the elevator to the underground parking garage. They'd come in her car, a sleek white Mercedes SLK convertible. Sure, it was a nice ride, but he wasn't a fan of the soft top. A bullet could easily tear through it, and a semi-automatic could cause some serious damage.

"It's not a good idea to go out," he said, as he opened the back door for her.

"It's only Robert," she said, climbing in. "He's not a threat."

Viper shut the door and climbed in behind the wheel. "It's

not that. It's just I can't guarantee your safety in a busy restaurant." And he sure as shit didn't want to sit and watch Robert wine and dine her. The guy was a jerk. He didn't care about Izzy, only about the company.

She leaned forward and put her hand on his shoulder. Just a brief touch, but it was enough to make him weak with longing. "I appreciate your concern, Viper, but it will be okay."

He put the vehicle into reverse, scanning the area. "It's my job to advise you on your security."

She smiled gently. "Consider me duly advised."

They left the tower block and headed back to her place. Her voice broke the silence. "Can you stop at a store? I've got nothing in the fridge."

He nodded, assessing their surroundings, and a short time later pulled up outside a mini supermarket. "Tell me what you want, and I'll go and get it. You wait here and keep the doors locked."

A soft sigh. "Okay, sure." She gave him a verbal list, then sat back, her mind elsewhere. The items were easy to find, and ten minutes later he was back in the car, driving her home.

He turned into her street and pulled over in front of her block. Luckily, there was a parking space right outside. Viper pulled in and turned off the engine. "I'll help you upstairs," he said, getting out of the car. Izzy opened her door and stepped out onto the sidewalk.

A black SUV crawled up the road.

Four-wheel drive. Blacked-out windows. No plates.

His senses went on high alert. "Izzy, get back in the car!"

She looked up, confused. The SUV sped up, its tires growling on the pavement. The side window opened, and the steel nozzle of an automatic pistol poked out.

"Get down!" Viper yelled, reaching for his gun.

Izzy dove back into the car, groceries spilling onto the street. She crouched low, her breath quickening.

The concierge stepped outside, concern etched on his face. Viper shouted for him to get back just as the shooter opened fire.

CHAPTER 33

Izzy screamed and covered her ears. The gunfire was deafening, echoing around her, bullets pinging into the car.

"Stay low!" Viper yelled over the chaos.

A bullet tore through the soft canopy of the convertible and embedded itself in the back of the seat where she'd been sitting moments before.

Holy hell. That was too close.

Why had she insisted on a convertible? No one had warned her it would be a risk in a shootout.

"Viper!"

He had maneuvered around to the other side of the car and was firing back. She could see him through the open door, his face a grim mask of concentration. His gun discharged in rapid succession, providing cover.

The noise was overwhelming.

The shooting seemed to last forever, but in reality, it was only a few seconds. She kept her head down, praying she wouldn't get hit.

Then, suddenly, silence. She heard the screech of tires as the SUV sped off down the road, disappearing around a bend.

"Quick, get out of the car!" Viper shouted, reaching for her.

Izzy grabbed his hand, letting him help her onto the sidewalk. They sprinted toward the front door. The concierge unlocked it, and they slipped inside. Viper kept his eyes on the road behind them.

"Is this bulletproof?" He tapped the thick glass with his gun.

"I don't know," said a stunned Lewis. He held a baseball bat, ready to swing if anyone came through the door. Izzy hoped that wouldn't be necessary.

"Call the cops," Viper barked. "Get them out here before that car comes back for another drive-by."

"Was that a warning, or did they mean to kill me?" Izzy couldn't stop shaking.

"Those weren't blanks they were shooting," Viper said. "That was for real."

"Oh, Lord." She sank down onto the tiled floor, her legs giving out. "Thank God you saw them coming."

He put his big, callused hand over hers. She fought the urge to cling to him, like she had in Mexico. "You're okay now."

She was alive, but only because of him. Tears threatened, but she blinked them away. Right now, she didn't care that their lives were different or that on paper it really shouldn't work. All she wanted was to be in his arms.

Biting her lip, she tried not to cry.

But she couldn't risk his job.

Lewis came back. "The police are on their way. I didn't get a look at them, did you?"

"One driver, one shooter," said Viper, matter-of-factly. "But I couldn't see their faces. They were wearing ski masks."

How had he noticed that? She hadn't even seen the SUV until it was right on them.

"There are security cameras outside this building," Lewis said helpfully. "The cops might be able to pick up something from that."

"Yeah, maybe. There were no plates on the vehicle."

Again, he'd noticed the finer details while she'd just cowered in the backseat.

"Only a handful of people knew you'd be here," Viper said, thinking out loud.

"From the meeting?"

He gave a tight nod. "They were waiting for you to show up."

A sob escaped her then. She couldn't help it; she was just so afraid. "I'm not safe anywhere. Should we go somewhere else? We could hide until this is over."

He hugged her then, enveloping her in his strong arms. "It'll be okay. I promise. You don't need to panic. We'll get these guys."

She clung to him, absorbing his steady presence, but didn't respond. She only hoped he was right. She wasn't sure how much more of this she could take.

AFTER THE POLICE had cordoned off the attack area, Viper retrieved the grocery bags and handed them to Lewis, who took them up to the apartment. He looked around, taking in every detail. The spent casings on the ground were from a 5.56 NATO round, typically used in M4 carbines.

He frowned. Different cartridges to the mercenaries who'd kidnapped Izzy.

"Did you see the shooters?" asked the officer in charge, a rugged, worn-looking cop who didn't bother to give his name.

Viper shook his head. "No, they wore masks."

"Did you get the make of the vehicle?"

"Yeah, it was a black Jeep. Couldn't tell you the model, though."

The cop scribbled in his notebook. "Thank you, sir. Since this is related to Miss Beaumont's kidnapping, a detective will be in touch in the next few hours."

Viper nodded. He knew the drill.

A silver BMW skidded to a halt outside the cordoned-off area, and Pat jumped out. "She okay?"

"Yeah, she's fine. Just a little rattled."

"Did you see anything?" Pat asked as they took the elevator up to the apartment.

Viper shook his head and told him the same thing he'd told the cop. Two men, black Jeep, no plates. Then he handed him the bullet casings. "Found these on the pavement."

Pat stared at them. "These are new."

"Yes, sir. They were waiting for her," he added as they got out of the elevator.

Pat huffed. "How the hell did they know she was back?"

"She was at a shareholder meeting this afternoon," Viper pointed out. "If they were watching the apartment, they could've seen us leave."

"Fuck, Viper. We have to catch these maniacs. This is getting dangerous."

Like it wasn't before.

Viper told him what Jackson Ferris had said about the two men captured in Mexico.

"I'll get onto my FBI contact and get him to go down there," Pat said, grimly. "Before the bastards go free."

As they entered the apartment, Viper couldn't relax. The grocery bags on the counter were a stark reminder of how quickly a mundane moment could turn deadly.

Izzy was sitting on the sofa, legs folded beneath her, sipping coffee. She looked up as they entered, her eyes flickering over Viper to rest on her uncle. "Pat, you didn't need to come."

"I wanted to check if you were okay."

She smiled. "I'm fine, just a little shaken up."

"Would you like some coffee, sir?" Viper asked.

"A cup would be great, thanks, Viper." Pat sat down in an armchair opposite Izzy. "The main thing is you're all right."

Viper poured the coffee and handed Pat a cup, then he sat down on the sofa beside Izzy.

"I'll get onto the authorities in Mexico City first thing tomorrow. If necessary, I'll fly out there myself and find out what's going on," Pat growled.

"I'm sorry to cause all this trouble," Izzy said.

"It's not your fault," Viper said automatically, then bit his tongue. Shit, he mustn't let on how well he knew Izzy. How familiar they were.

Pat nodded. "Viper's right. This has got to do with the mine, not you. It's not your fault you inherited it. But to be honest, Izzy, and don't take this the wrong way, but you might want to consider selling your stake in the company."

She gave a small nod. "I have been thinking about it. I broached it with the board earlier today."

"And?"

"They weren't happy. Both Robert and Raf tried to talk me out of it."

"A change of ownership means they'll be out of a job."

"Yeah, but they'll get a great deal. I can't do this forever, I'm not cut out for it."

Viper was glad she'd come to that decision. The stress was getting to her.

"This is not your problem," Pat agreed. "Companies are bought and sold all the time." Pat had a point.

Izzy nodded. "I know, you're right. I realized that to support the local community, the company needs a strong leader at the helm. Someone who understands the business and wants to be there."

"Robert?" Pat asked.

"No, not Robert. He's done a great job, but he barely goes to the mine. Raf hasn't ever been down there."

"Who then?" Pat tilted his head.

"I've had several offers that I'm considering."

"Good. Let someone else take it on. It's become too dangerous and it can't be doing your social media profile any good."

Viper hadn't even considered that. These attempts on her life would cause her sponsors to worry. They might even decide she wasn't worth the risk.

She threw her hands in the air. "You're right, they are getting antsy. They want me back, and at the moment, I'm too scared to stick my head outside the door."

"We'll get to the bottom of this," Pat said, getting to his feet. "I've got to get back to the office, but Viper will look after you. Call me if you need anything."

"I'll see you out." Izzy handed her cup to Viper, then put her hand on his thigh to push herself up.

Viper froze.

Pat's gaze flickered, but he didn't comment. "I'll be in touch."

Fuck. Fuck. Fuck!

He knew.

That one small gesture had given the game away. It had

been so casual, so natural, that of course it meant something. Izzy hadn't even realized she'd done it.

She saw him out, then turned and noticed the expression on his face. "What?"

He stared at her, rigid with shock.

She gasped, and her hand flew to her mouth. "Oh, crap!"

CHAPTER 34

"I'm so sorry." Izzy couldn't believe what she'd done. "I didn't think."

"It's okay." Viper paced up and down the room.

But it wasn't. She could see it wasn't. Viper had turned pale, and for the first time since she'd met him, he looked scared. Terrorists, bullets, and mercenaries didn't frighten him, but the prospect of losing his job did.

He'd tried to warn her. They'd even clarified that there was nothing happening between them, because he was afraid of Pat finding out. And she'd gone and screwed it up.

"Are you sure he knows?"

He gave a helpless nod. "I saw it in his face."

Shit.

"What do you think he'll do?" she whispered.

"I don't know, but there are consequences for getting romantically involved with your principal and I'm on a probation period." He sank down onto the sofa and dropped his head into his hands.

She felt so bad. "What if we deny it?"

He glanced up, and she saw just how wretched he looked.

"You touched my thigh. That wasn't an accidental gesture. He'll know I'm lying and that's even worse. I'm not going to lie to my commanding officer."

"Okay, then I'll talk to Pat," she said. "This is my fault. I'll sort it out."

His face softened for a brief moment. "I appreciate you're trying to help, but there's nothing you can do. Rules are rules. I'm going to have to face the music."

On cue, his phone beeped.

He took it out of his pocket and looked at it.

"Is that him?" she whispered.

"Yeah." His eyes were haunted. "He wants to see me first thing tomorrow morning."

"I suppose it won't help if I tell him there's nothing between us anymore." Izzy was grasping at straws, but there must be something she could do. She'd known Pat her whole life. He wasn't a mean person. Surely, he wouldn't fire Viper when he knew this job meant so much to him.

Besides, she was as much to blame as he was. If not more. She'd asked him to hold her that first night. She'd instigated the affair between them. She would just have to make sure he didn't get fired because of it.

"I'm so sorry," Izzy said again, feeling the weight of her guilt.

Viper stopped pacing and looked at her, his eyes filled with a mix of fear and resignation. "I know you are."

She nodded, but inside, she was determined to do whatever it took to make things right. She couldn't let Viper lose everything because of her mistake.

* * *

"I DON'T NEED to tell you why you're here," Pat said, once

Viper was seated in his office. There was an edge of steel to his voice that terrified him.

"No, sir."

Pat sighed. "I know what it's like, Viper, and she's a beautiful girl, but you know the rules."

"I know. I'm sorry, sir. If it's any consolation, it's over between us. I ended it as soon as we got back to D.C."

Pat studied him. His dark gaze was hard to read. "Do you have feelings for her?"

"Yes, sir."

"Real feelings, or is this just something that happened on the job?"

There was no point in denying it. "Real feelings, sir."

Pat sighed. "Goddamn it, Viper. You know I've got to take you off the case."

Viper frowned. "Is that really necessary?"

"You damn well know it is. You're too close. I need someone with a clear head protecting her. Not someone who's going to be ogling her rather than keeping lookout."

Viper stared at the floor. His boss was right. Even in Mexico they'd been caught by surprise by that German mining executive who'd snuck up from the beach. Because he hadn't been doing his job properly. He'd been strolling hand-in-hand with Izzy and hadn't noticed the threat.

"I understand, sir."

"I wish it wasn't so, Viper, but as of now I'm assigning someone else to guard Izzy."

"Am I fired, sir? I know this was only a probationary position."

Pat paused. The tension drew out. There were very few men that could make him feel uncomfortable, but Pat was one of them.

"I'm not sure yet," he finally said. "We're so busy, and now I have to put someone else on Izzy, I could use you. I'll get

Anna to reassign you. Grab your things from Izzy's apartment and come straight back here. No lingering goodbyes, okay? I need your butt back at work."

"Yes, sir."

He felt weak with relief. At least he still had a job. If he could prove himself to Pat and stay away from Izzy, then he might just be able to keep it.

CHAPTER 35

The new bodyguard was as professional as Viper had been. He answered, "Yes, ma'am," to every-thing she said, unless he was talking to her about security, in which case it was Miss Beaumont. He was a fine-looking man, big, strong, like they all were. But he wasn't Viper.

Emily came around early the next morning, bustling with energy. "Oh, my God, Iz, what the heck is going on? First the kidnapping, now a drive-by shooting. These guys aren't messing around, are they?"

"No, they're not," she mumbled. She hadn't slept well without Viper's arms around her, and not having him here made her realize how much she missed him. She hadn't spoken to him since he'd come back for his things after his meeting with Pat. Even then, their exchange had been brief.

"I've got to go," he'd said, once he'd packed his meager belongings into a backpack. "Pat's expecting me back at work."

"Okay, sure. If you must go."

There'd been no hug, no kiss, no nothing other than a stiff

goodbye and a "see ya." Then he'd walked out of her apartment and her life.

"Well, since you can't go out and we can't shoot you for your channel," Emily was saying, "I've arranged for Lara to come to you."

Lara was a local photographer, an expert in social media shoots.

"What, here?"

She spread her arms. "Why not? We've done photoshoots at your place before. You've got plenty of natural light and that lovely wide balcony. Izzy recuperating at home. Izzy looking stunning in this year's fall must-haves." She grinned. "That'll keep them happy—just until you can get back out there."

At her lackluster expression, Emily said, "What's wrong with you? I know you've been through hell lately, but you're always so enthusiastic about your business." She paused and cocked her head to the side. "Is this about him?"

"Who?"

Emily tilted her head. "Come on, Iz. How long have we known each other?"

She sighed. "Honestly, Em. There's nothing going on between me and Viper." Not anymore.

"Are you sure? Because I've never seen you this down."

"It's just the stress getting to me."

Emily squeezed her hand. "I can't imagine how you must be feeling. I was scared just entering the building."

"Thanks."

"Sorry, I know that's not helping. Shall I schedule Lara for tomorrow? It might do you good to have something else to focus on."

She had a point. It would take her mind off Viper.

"Yes, okay. Tomorrow's fine."

"Great." Emily fired off a text message. "Now that's out of

the way, shall we have a glass of wine and I'll update you on everything that's been happening."

The afternoon sped by. They drank most of the bottle as Emily filled her in on the new brands that wanted to work with her, the orders from her swimsuit line, the marketing around her new collection, and the other ventures she'd begun investigating.

The sun was setting when Izzy's phone beeped.

"Oh, crap," she murmured. "I'm having dinner with Robert tonight."

"Robert?" Emily raised an eyebrow. "I thought you weren't interested in him?"

"I'm not, but we need to talk."

"It'll probably do you good. I don't like the thought of you moping here by yourself all evening."

"I'm not supposed to leave the apartment."

"Let him come to you, then." Emily had an answer for everything. "Tell him to stop by Del Posto on the way and pick up something nice."

Izzy perked up a bit. "Yes, we could do that. At least then I wouldn't have to get dressed up."

"You really are out of sorts," Emily said, frowning. "Cheer up, I'm sure they'll catch who's doing this soon."

"I hope so." She had visions of having to look over her shoulder for the rest of her life, or at least until she'd sold her share in the company. The more she thought about it, the more she decided Pat was right. Her heart wasn't in Omega Enterprises. As much as she cared about the communities the project supported in Mexico, the company wasn't her primary focus. It deserved to be in the hands of someone who really cared about it.

Someone who knew what they were doing.

Not her.

She was just winging it, grasping onto the reins because

she was trying to maintain the status quo. But that wasn't working. Her life and her livelihood were now at risk. She didn't want to get any more involved in the company than she was, which put more strain on Robert and Raf. In the end, it was probably better that she get out.

When Emily had left, she texted Robert and explained that she couldn't leave the apartment and asked if he minded coming here. He agreed and said he'd pick up something on the way over.

Then, she had a long bath and tried not to think about Viper. As she got dressed in a floor-length maxi dress with a light cardigan, she tried not to think about how it felt in his arms. And as she blow-dried her hair, she tried not to think about how it felt when he ran his fingers through it.

Damn, this wasn't getting any easier. Still, it had only been a day. It would take some time to get him out of her system. She had to be a big girl about it; she had a business to run, another business to sell, and her own life to take care of now that he was gone.

Robert would be here soon. There was one more thing she had to do before he arrived. She picked up her phone and called Pat.

"It wasn't his fault, you know." She could hear Radiohead playing in the background and knew he was at home. An old memory of lying on the rug with his son, Joe, listening to Pat's rock collection flashed through her mind. They'd been in their teens then. It seemed like a lifetime ago.

"It doesn't matter whose fault it is, Izzy. I can't have him distracted on the job. It's too important. Your safety is too important."

"He's saved my life more times than I care to remember," she pointed out. "That should tell you something."

"It does, and Viper's a damn good operative, but he broke the rules."

She sighed. "It was me who started it. None of this was his fault. You're punishing him for something I did."

"I've taken him off your protection detail, Izzy. I haven't fired him."

"You're not going to, are you?"

"No, I'm not. I can't afford to lose him. I'm under-resourced right now."

She smiled fondly. Pat was so transparent.

"Okay, good." There was a pause. "How are things going?"

"Busy. But that's a good thing."

"Pat..." She paused. "Could we get together sometime and talk about Mom?"

There was a moment of silence, then he cleared his throat. "Sure we can. Do you want me to come over now?"

"I can't tonight. Robert's coming over for dinner."

"Oh, I see."

She heard the surprise in his voice. "It's not like that. I need to talk to him about my plans for the company. I've decided to take your advice and get out."

"I think that's wise," he restated. "How will Robert take it?"

"He won't like it. It puts his position at risk. With me in charge, he has free rein of the company. I think he was hoping to buy me out himself one day."

"Well, you gotta do what you gotta do," said Pat. "You have to do what's right for you."

"I know." Suddenly, all she wanted to do was sell her share in the company and put this mess behind her so she could get on with her life. She didn't kid herself that there was any hope for her and Viper. After what she'd done, he wouldn't come near her again. And anyway, how would a rough-around-the-edges soldier with scars on his hands and eyes the color of the ocean fit into her schedule?

Would he even want to?

The whirl of the fashion industry. The glamorous parties. The social media following.

It just wasn't him.

She sighed as she applied some blush and lip gloss. At least she had the memories.

A week of blissful passion in a tropical resort. An affair born out of danger and fear, but so beautiful and so comforting at the same time. A dream she would always remember.

The doorbell rang.

She stood up, checked her reflection, and plastered a smile on her face. Time to face Robert.

CHAPTER 36

Viper got back home around six. He'd been part of a team of men hired to guard a Chinese delegation that had arrived in D.C. for a series of important meetings. He wasn't point, but backup, equipped with an earpiece and following in a discreet SUV along with two police motorcyclists.

Now the delegation was firmly ensconced at their hotel, they'd handed over to a different team for the night shift.

With nothing to do, he paced up and down his living room and thought about Izzy. Was she okay? Did she miss him as much as he missed her? Fuck, he wanted to hold her so bad it hurt.

As he stared out of the window at his overgrown garden, he ignored the knot in his chest. Izzy was in her penthouse apartment, surrounded by stylists and photographers. He was in his run-down house in Fredericksburg, alone. The strange thing was, he'd never needed more than this.

Until now.

He sighed. They were polar opposites. It would never

have worked. Except what they'd had, that had been real. He'd never felt that way about anyone before.

Fuck it.

He got a beer from the fridge, turned on the television, and sank onto the sofa. The channel it was on was playing reruns of Shark Tank. He watched as two of the judges agreed to invest in the start-up. Equal share. They'd each be putting in twenty-five percent of the capital.

Viper stared at the TV. Something Izzy had said came back to him.

A cold shiver ran down his spine.

Shit.

Of course.

He jumped off the sofa. Suddenly, he knew who'd attacked her outside her apartment—or at least, he thought he did.

Viper grabbed his leather motorcycle jacket and ran outside. His Suzuki SF250 superbike was resting on its stand in the parking lot. He jumped on, put on his helmet and started the engine. The motorcycle woke up with a low growl.

He revved it just to get the juices flowing, it had been a while since he'd taken her for a ride. Then, he zoomed out of the parking lot and down the road.

IT TOOK him just under an hour to get to D.C. As he turned into the crescent street in which Izzy lived, his pulse increased. He drove slowly past, checking out the front of the building. It was lit up, the outside lights elegantly illuminating the front steps and the two stylish potted plants on either side of the glass doors.

Where was the cop?

The Metropolitan Police Department was supposed to have an officer outside the door, but he couldn't see anyone.

Viper pulled over, took out his phone, and called Pat.

"First Izzy, and now you," growled the former SEAL Commander into the phone. "This had better be good."

"Sir, has the police presence been recalled from Izzy's apartment?"

A pause.

"No, not that I know of. Why?"

"Because I'm outside now and I can't see anyone."

"For fuck's sake, Viper, what are you doing there? Do you *want* me to fire you?"

"I had an idea, sir, about who was responsible for today's attempt on her life, so I came by to check and there is nobody guarding the place."

"You're sure?"

Viper got off his bike and placed the helmet on the seat. "Yeah. Hold on, I'm going to take a closer look." As a precaution, he drew his gun.

Just in case.

Apart from the streetlamps and the lights above the front entrance, the road was in darkness. He walked up and down outside the building, but there was nobody around. The park opposite seemed deserted too.

Then he heard a low moan.

"I've got something," he hissed into the receiver, before jumping over the low fence that surrounded the park. "Hello?"

"What is it?" Pat asked urgently in his ear. "Do you need backup?"

Viper saw boots sticking out of a nearby bush. He rushed over and bent down. The police officer was lying on his back, moaning.

"Man down. Man down," said Viper urgently. "The officer

has been shot. Gunshot wound to the stomach. He's in the park. Alive, but only just."

"I'll send the paramedics," Pat barked. "What about Izzy?"

Viper heard the worry in his voice. "I'm going to check on her now."

He raced back across the road and leaped up the front steps to the building. The front doors were locked, so he pounded on the glass.

Where the hell was Lewis?

Then he saw the pool of blood on the marble floor, and he went cold.

Fuck.

If Lewis was injured, possibly dead, what did that mean for Izzy? He pushed her buzzer, but there was no response. Heart pounding, he pressed every buzzer on the pad.

Come on. Somebody let me in.

Nothing.

The intruders must have disconnected the intercom system. There was no time to waste. Viper aimed his gun at the lock and blew a hole in it.

The sound reverberated around the building. Viper kicked the door open and dashed inside. Lewis was lying behind the front desk, pressing down on a bullet hole in his leg, trying to stem the bleeding. His face was ashen.

"They went up to her apartment," he rasped.

"How long?" Viper demanded, running past. He wished he could stop and help the concierge, but... Izzy.

"Ten minutes ago."

"Help is coming," Viper called, heading for the stairwell. "Keep pressure on that wound." He took the stairs two at a time and ran all the way up.

If they'd hurt her...

He couldn't bear to think about that.

Shit! Why hadn't he seen this sooner? He ought to have realized.

He'd been so stupid. It had been staring them in the face all the time. Izzy had said as much herself.

He'd lose everything if I sold out.

Then on the yacht: *I wanted to take it to the next level.*

It was only after seeing that program that he'd put two and two together. He didn't bother ringing the bell, he simply shot out the lock and kicked the door open. His replacement was lying unconscious on the kitchen floor, a nasty gash at the back of his head. Viper bent down to feel his pulse. He was alive.

"Izzy!" he shouted.

No reply.

An icy dread gripped him as he raced into the bedroom. It was empty. So was the spare room, and her study. Where the fuck was she?

They'd taken her somewhere. That wasn't good. But if she was in transit, at least it meant she was still alive. There was still time to get to her. If they'd killed her, they would have left her body here. He felt sick to the stomach. He had to find her.

Ten minutes, Lewis had said. That wasn't long. They might still be in the building.

The parking garage!

That's where they'd have parked their vehicle. Out of sight of the road. Somewhere you could lead a struggling woman without anyone seeing you.

He charged back down the stairs, jumping the last few on every landing, before pushing open the door to the underground parking garage.

The concrete flooring and open sides let in the cold, dark air, but it was well lit. He stopped and listened for any signs of activity.

Footsteps. A car door.

Then a muffled scream.

Izzy!

He followed the sound to the far corner of the parking garage. A black SUV stood with its doors open, and two men leaning into the back.

"Izzy!" he shouted.

The men glanced up.

"Viper, help!"

He launched into a sprint.

One of the men opened fire. The bullet whizzed past his head. He heard it embed itself into the concrete pillar beside him, but he didn't slow down.

"Let's go!" shouted a male voice.

Doors slammed and the car growled to life. The tires screeched as the SUV pulled out of the parking space. The window rolled down and Viper saw the barrel of a rifle.

More shots were fired, but they were erratic, the shooter not having time to aim.

Viper figured the odds were in his favor. He sprinted after the vehicle, knowing that he had to get to Izzy before they took off with her. There was no doubt in his mind that they planned to kill her and dump her body where it would leave no trace.

"Izzy!" he yelled.

Then he gasped and flew backward as the wind was knocked out of him. It was hard to breathe. He looked down and realized he'd been shot.

CHAPTER 37

*V*iper lay on the ground, groaning, gun still in his hand.

He was still alive! And amazingly, there was no blood. He felt under his shirt and saw the Kevlar vest had taken the bullet.

Thank God!

It had just winded him.

The SUV was hurtling toward the ramp leading out of the parking garage. Rolling onto his side, he fired at the wheels. The back one exploded and the car tilted onto its side before it rolled over and smashed into a pillar. The hood crumpled like an accordion and steam hissed out.

Izzy.

Viper got to his feet, a little unsteadily, then stumbled toward the car wreck.

The air bags had deployed and the two men in the front were bent forward, unconscious. He pulled open the back door.

Izzy lay scrunched in a ball on the back seat. Her hands

and feet were bound, and duct tape covered her mouth. When she saw him, her eyes filled with tears.

He reached in. "Izzy, are you okay?"

At first glance she seemed okay, but he couldn't be sure. Her eyes were open but there was a large bruise on her cheek and some dried blood on her neck.

He grabbed his knife and cut the plastic ties around her wrists and ankles, then he gently peeled the tape off her mouth.

"Viper! Oh, God, Viper. It was Robert. Robert and Raf. They were in it together."

He nodded. "I know. I just figured it out."

There was a cut on her lip, but it had stopped bleeding. That jerk Robert must have hit her.

Going around to the front of the vehicle, he wrenched open the driver's door. Robert lay slumped over the air bag, groaning. He was in a bad way. Blood poured down his face from a nasty gash on his forehead, mixing with that dripping from his nose.

Raf was still out cold.

Robert tried to sit up, but Viper grabbed the gun from his limp hand and pointed it at his head. "One move and you're dead, you fucking prick."

Robert blinked at him through unfocused eyes and grunted something inaudible.

In the distance, they heard sirens. Moments later, police officers burst through the elevator entrance, and Pat's silver BMW, followed by a blaring police vehicle, raced down the ramp into the underground parking garage.

The vehicles screeched to a halt beside the car wreck, diesel fumes filling the confined space.

"Jesus, Izzy!" Pat ran toward her. "Are you okay?"

Viper helped him lift Izzy out of the car, while several armed officers pointed guns at the two injured kidnappers.

* * *

"How did you know?" Izzy asked Viper, once he'd sat her down in Pat's car and wrapped his jacket around her shoulders. The leather still held the heat from his body, and it smelled of his aftershave.

"That's what I'd like to know," Pat muttered.

Viper cleared his throat. "I was watching TV when it hit me. Robert had the most to lose if you sold the mine, and he was trying to win you over. He would have married you to get a controlling share of the mine."

"I don't understand," she said. "My share wouldn't go to him just because we were married."

"My guess is that he would have arranged a little "accident" shortly after your wedding. A hit-and-run, or something similar. As your husband, he'd inherit everything."

Izzy stared at him, aghast. Even Pat looked shocked. "You really think that was his plan?"

Viper turned to Izzy. "Think about it. He's been dating you for months, trying to take your relationship to the next level. It was only today, when you told him you weren't interested in him, that he realized his cunning plan wasn't going to work. That's when he organized the drive-by shooting."

"But, if I die, Raf will inherit my share of the company, not him," Izzy said.

"Exactly. That's how I knew they had to be in it together. They obviously made a pact. The best-case scenario was for Robert to marry you and gain control that way. When that didn't work, he brought in Raf, and they struck a deal. He'd get rid of you for a percentage of the company."

"I can't believe Raf agreed to that." Her head was spinning. This was totally unbelievable. Robert, who she'd trusted, and Raf, her own cousin.

"Well, they risked losing everything when you told them you were thinking about selling," Viper said. "They had to act fast."

"They must have had those drive-by hitmen primed and ready," said Pat, his jaw tense.

Izzy felt a chill run down her spine and pulled the jacket tighter around her. "It feels so unreal. When I told Robert I'd met with a buyer, he lost it. He knocked out the bodyguard and tied me up. Then Raf came in, and they carried me to the car. I can't believe they were going to kill me."

"No doubt about it," Viper said firmly.

She winced. "To think I made Robert CEO when my father died." Her eyes widened. "Do you think Robert was responsible for his death too?"

"No," said Pat, immediately. "That was the cartel."

Viper arched an eyebrow. "Did the suspects confess?"

He gave a curt nod. "One of the FBI agents flew down there this afternoon, and they struck a deal with one of the suspects for information on the cartel."

Izzy leaned forward. "What did he say?"

"The leader of the cartel ordered the hit on Richard. Once the U.S. authorities recover his vehicle from the ravine, they expect to find evidence that he was forced off the road."

Izzy bit her lip. "Oh, my God." It was a lot to take in. "Then when I took over, they decided to kidnap me in exchange for the mining rights."

"That's about it," Pat confirmed.

"What about now?"

"Sell the company and it's no longer your problem," Pat said.

Izzy nodded. "I still can't believe they were willing to take me out." She wasn't talking about the cartel anymore. "My father entrusted the company to Robert, and Raf was given the shares by his father. How could they do this?"

"Your uncle wasn't a very savory person," said Pat quietly.

Izzy stared at him. "You knew Uncle Pete?"

"Yeah, I met him once or twice at your folks' house. The first time, he was asking for money. Your father sent him packing. There was a nasty fight outside. Richard punched him and the neighbors called the cops. I managed to calm everyone down and no charges were filed."

Izzy was shocked. "I had no idea."

"The second was a few years later. They'd reconciled and Peter asked that Raf be given a stake in the company. He'd just graduated with an MBA from Georgetown. Your father agreed, because it wasn't the kid's fault his father was a conman and a loser."

"Raf never mentioned his parents."

"Understandable. Anyway, after that, Raf started working at the company and despite your father's misgivings, he did well."

"I remember when he started," Izzy said. "What happened to his father?"

"Peter had disappeared by then. I think he owed some dangerous people a great deal of money, and his wife refused to bail him out. They subsequently divorced."

"How do you know so much about my family?" Izzy asked Pat.

He shrugged. "I told you, your mother and I were close. We talked. She told me things."

Izzy felt the trauma of the last few hours start to catch up with her. "I'd love to hear more, but right now I just want to go upstairs and rest." She glanced at Viper. "Will you take me home?"

She saw Viper glance at Pat, who nodded. "You'll have to go down to the precinct tomorrow and give your statement. I'll stay here and clear up this mess."

"I will, and by the way, Viper is staying with me tonight, whether you like it or not."

Pat's dark eyes sparkled. "Since he's no longer your personal protection officer, I don't have a problem with that."

Viper exhaled. Thank God for that, because he was about to tell Pat he could go to hell. Izzy needed him and he wasn't about to let her down.

Not after this. Not for anyone.

CHAPTER 38

"What happened to my front door?" Izzy gasped, as Viper helped her into her apartment.

"Oh, yeah. Sorry about that. I couldn't get in, so I shot it."

She wrapped her arms around his neck. "I don't care about the door. I'm just grateful you got here when you did. You saved my life. Again."

"Hopefully, this will be the last time."

Now that he was back, she didn't want to let him go. "I've missed you."

"I've missed you too. I'm sorry for leaving without saying a proper goodbye. I panicked. I didn't want to risk—"

"Shh…" She kissed him gently on the lips. "I know how important this job is to you. I would never knowingly jeopardize that."

He took her face in his hand. "You don't think you can kiss me like that then stop, do you?"

She smirked. "I was trying to get you to shut up. I've had enough talking—"

He kissed her this time, effectively cutting her off. She

moaned softly as he delved into her mouth, sliding his tongue against hers. God, she loved kissing him.

It deepened, became more intoxicating, until they were both gasping for breath. Deftly, Viper picked her up and carried her into the bedroom.

"I've been wanting to do this ever since we got back from Mexico," he said, dropping her gently onto the king-size bed.

He wasn't joking. She glanced up and saw him straining against his trousers.

"Me too," she whispered.

He took off his shirt, dropping it onto the floor. The Kevlar vest hugged him like a suit of armor. Izzy stared at it. "Oh, my God. Is that a bullet?"

"Yeah, lucky I was wearing this. I grabbed it at the last moment, thinking it might come in handy." He tore it off and tossed it onto the bed.

Izzy fingered the bullet, compressed into the vest. To think that could have been in his chest.

He took it from her and put it on the floor. "I forgot about that. The CSI team will want to have a look at that."

"You forgot you'd been shot?"

He shrugged. "I was trying to get to you."

Trembling, she reached up to him. "You could have died."

He lowered himself into her arms. "But I didn't."

Tears welled and she couldn't stop them. "I love you, Viper Morgan. I don't know if you know that, but you should by now."

He nuzzled her, his voice a husky whisper in her ear. "You should know that I love you, Miss Beaumont."

She giggled. "I had hoped that was the case."

He ran his finger over the bruise on her cheek. "Did he hurt you?"

She shook her head. "Nothing I couldn't handle."

"That's my girl."

He lowered his head and reclaimed her mouth, picking up where they'd left off. Izzy wrapped herself around him, feeling every muscle in his hard, toned body. Her hands ran over his ripped shoulders and down his sculpted back. This was her hero, her savior, her Navy SEAL, and master of her heart.

No matter how many times he'd rescued her, he'd also captured her body and soul, and she didn't want to ever let him go. Sure, they had different lives, but none of that mattered now.

They were together, and that was the main thing.

He rolled over and pulled her on top of him. Deftly, he unzipped the back of her dress. She shimmied out of it, kicking it onto the floor. Next, he unhooked her bra, letting her breasts fall free.

His hands slid down her sides, making her shiver with delight, as his thumbs hooked under her panties and helped her wriggle out of them. Naked, she lay on top of him, reveling in the feel of his hardness beneath hers.

He slid her up and suckled her breast, teasing her nipple with his tongue. God, that felt incredible. Then he switched to the other, until she was a hot, writhing mess. This man made her feel things nobody else did.

Her body was on fire, screaming to feel him inside of her.

She straddled him, aware he was watching her with his sea-blue eyes. Her breath quickened as she held his gaze. Slowly, she lowered herself on top of him. He inhaled sharply as she sank down, encasing him fully.

His head dropped back, and she relished the feeling of fullness as she sat on top of him, his swollen cock buried deep inside her.

With a moan, she began to move. Craving the friction as she slid back and forth, her hands on his chest.

His muscles flexed beneath her. "God, Izzy..."

He was watching her again, this time with a look of wonder on his face.

A surge of warmth spread through her body. It grew, hotter and hotter, until she felt like she was going to spontaneously combust.

He bucked as she rode him, maximizing the contact, allowing her to be penetrated fully with each mind-blowing stroke. Her breath came in small gasps as the feeling of fullness grew.

"Oh, God," she moaned, her hips jerking spasmodically on top of him. "Oh, shit, Viper."

He held her tight, his fingertips pressing into her butt cheeks, pulling her forward and back in time to her rhythm. The veins stood out on his forehead, and his chest heaved with each thrust.

The fullness grew until she couldn't stand it anymore. She began to cry out with each stroke. Finally, it reached a peak and shattered in one glorious explosion. Izzy screamed and clutched at his chest as she rocked back and forth on top of him.

He growled her name and gripped her tightly, pinning her down on top of him. His hot explosion sent her flying over another precipice, and she cried out as she contracted against him, over and over again, spasms of pleasure firing through her body. Heat that only he could give her.

Quivering, she clung to him as they both rode out the waves of their climax. Finally, when the shudders had subsided, she collapsed onto him, her body damp with perspiration.

"I feel like my heart is going to burst," she whispered, her face wet with tears.

He took her hand and placed it over his chest. It thumped manically. "Mine's the same."

She looked into his eyes and saw her own feelings

reflected there. That's when she knew everything was going to be all right. Yes, they were different, but that didn't mean they weren't suited. There was nobody else in the entire world she wanted to be with.

Whatever their differences, they'd overcome them.

EPILOGUE

hree weeks later.

"How's the sale going?" Pat asked Izzy.

They were sitting in Pat's living room drinking sodas and talking. Aside from his apartment in D.C. he had a house in Fayetteville, close to Fort Bragg where he'd served for so many years. Viper had driven them there on his motorcycle, much to his boss's disapproval.

"It was my idea," Izzy had said, when they'd walked in carrying helmets.

Viper had shaken Pat's hand, ignoring the scowl.

Izzy smiled. "It's going well. I spoke to Gert Henderson from GHMG Holdings yesterday and he's meeting with me tomorrow to finalize the details. In a few more days, Omega Enterprises will be under new management."

"That's great news."

"Yeah, and Gert has agreed to keep it operating as normal until they expand production. That means they'll keep on the local employees as well as Hernández's security company, who've done such a great job protecting the mine."

"Henderson was a good choice," said Viper. Even if at first the eccentric mining magnate had startled them with his sudden appearance in the hotel gardens.

"It's the best thing for you," said Pat.

Viper still felt weird seeing his boss socially, but since he and Izzy were officially dating, it couldn't really be avoided. He knew Pat would be watching closely, so he had to be on his best behavior. There were also operational concerns, but he and Pat had already had a long chat about those.

"I'm looking forward to getting back to my business, now that this nightmare is over." She grasped Viper's hand. He squeezed it back. They'd barely spent a night apart since he'd shot the tires out of Robert's car and rescued her. He still couldn't believe this beautiful, glamorous, stunning woman was really his. That the dreamlike week in Mexico was now a reality. Plus, he never tired of kissing her until she gasped for air or making love to her until she screamed his name.

Every day with Izzy was an adventure. Her schedule was grueling, and she worked harder than anyone he'd ever met, but when she looked at him in that way, his heart leaped with joy. Like it was doing now.

"You must have a lot of work to catch up on?" Pat said.

She shrugged. "I'm getting a handle on it already. Emily's amazing. She's kept things going for me, so I'm not drowning in emails."

"What about you?" Pat asked Viper. "How are you coping? Keeping out of the press?"

"So far, yes."

They'd decided not to mention his part in Izzy's rescue to keep the media attention around him to a minimum. Not much was known about Izzy Beaumont's brawny new boyfriend except he was a war veteran.

"I tell anyone that asks that we met in San Diego," she smiled, her eyes sparkling. "He was there on a guys' trip, we met in a bar and hit it off."

Pat nodded. "Good. If the world knows who you are, it will seriously compromise your ability to work for the unit."

They'd been through this before. After the Colombia terror attack, the military secured a press injunction to keep his identity under wraps. Revealing it would put not just his life at risk, but also those around him. Foreign terror groups would jump at the chance to capture a former Navy SEAL.

"It won't be easy keeping a low profile with Izzy around." Pat smiled fondly at his goddaughter.

"You'd be surprised," she laughed. "It's not that bad. Outside of the social media shoots, I live a fairly quiet life."

"Well, I'm happy for you both." Pat got up and walked toward a photograph in a silver frame on the mantelpiece. Viper had seen it when he'd walked in. It was a beautiful one of Richard and Astrid Beaumont, with Izzy in front of them. They were all smiling at the camera, happy in that moment. Izzy's mother had indeed been a beauty. She had Izzy's dark hair, heart-shaped face and wide smile.

He paused to study it. "Your mother would be so proud of you."

"I wish she were here now," Izzy murmured, her eyes on the photograph.

Pat turned around. "I know, but you still have me, and now you've got Viper, as well. We're your family."

She smiled. "That's the only photograph I've seen of me and my parents together."

Pat handed it to her. "You have it."

She took it and smiled at the image of the happy family. "I'll make a copy."

Viper looked at the photo in Izzy's hands. Both Izzy's parents had blue eyes. Hers were brown. He frowned, trying to remember his high school biology. Wasn't that a genetic impossibility?

"I remember this day," Izzy was saying. "It was in the summer and my father was back home. We went to the beach and ate ice cream and swam in the ocean. It was a good day."

Viper glanced up to find Pat's eyes on him. Intense, chocolate-brown eyes that could harden to black in a nanosecond. Izzy had those same eyes.

He opened his mouth to say something when Pat gave a tiny shake of his head. Viper hesitated. Had he imagined that?

He frowned, confused. There it was again. A minuscule shake that said...

Don't.

"It's a beautiful photograph," Viper said, questions whirling through his mind. "You should definitely have a copy."

Pat's shoulders dropped in relief.

No fucking way. Pat was Izzy's biological father.

Viper sat back and sipped his beer. How had no one figured that out before? Izzy was talking about Joe now, and how they used to listen to Pat's old records. The former SEAL Commander smiled sadly at the memory of his son. A true hero, who'd died on the battlefield.

For some reason, Pat didn't want Izzy to know he was her father. Viper respected that. He wouldn't say anything. It wasn't his secret to tell.

When the time was right, Pat would tell Izzy—or not. Perhaps out of respect for her parents or his late wife, he wouldn't say anything.

They finished their drinks and got up to leave. Pat walked them to the door where he hugged Izzy. "I really am happy for you."

"Thanks, Uncle Pat."

Then he shook Viper's hand. "Thank you."

Viper nodded. Pat didn't have to say anymore. His secret was safe.

"Pat is such a sweetheart," said Izzy, when they got back home. "One day I must ask him how he and my mother met."

Viper took her into his arms and smiled at her. "I think that's an excellent idea."

FORBIDDEN ACCESS

BLACKTHORN SECURITY - BOOK 4

CHAPTER 1

This was a terrible idea.

She'd known it from the moment she'd been handed this assignment, but her instructions were clear: "Clayton is instrumental to the US government, a High Value Target who must be protected at all costs."

As she parked her car down the road from the Lydian building, she let out an unladylike snort. The guy was a criminal. His technology fueled illegal activities on the dark web. People had died because of him.

Okay, that hadn't been proven, but the dark web was a cesspool of illicit dealings: weapons, human trafficking, money laundering, and terrorism funding.

Why the hell were they protecting this guy?

But she knew why.

He was helping the NSA trace illegal transactions tied to terrorist groups, including those orchestrated by an arms dealer named Aleksandar Markov. Markov had been a person of interest to the U.S. authorities for years, but nobody could pin anything on him. Now, with Clayton's revolutionary new upgrade, they might be able to tie him—and a host of other bad guys—into any number of crimes.

That meant Clayton had a big red target on his head.

She scowled as she pulled her skirt down and tried to march in these ridiculous heels toward the front entrance of the building. She hoped to hell she wouldn't have to make a quick getaway, because she wouldn't get very far before falling flat on her face.

Better for everyone if Damian Clayton and his shady cryptocurrency vanished, but that wasn't up to her.

Since joining Blackthorn Security as a private operator, she'd traded her life as an undercover operative for lucrative private security contracts. Pat, the resourceful ex-SEAL Commander and her new boss, had the inside track to government operations, ensuring his agency handled off-the-books missions for national security. Rose preferred it to a mundane job on Civvie Street.

"Why the sudden change of heart?" she'd asked, back at the office. Cryptocurrency Developers weren't known for their altruism or government cooperation.

"He had an attack of conscience," Pat had replied, offering no further explanation.

Rose scoffed.

An attack of conscience, my ass.

People like Clayton didn't change. They didn't suddenly wake up and think, I don't want to do this anymore. I think I'll turn myself in, cut a deal and go on the straight and narrow.

The authorities obviously had something on him, and were willing to overlook it, in exchange for his cooperation.

The Lydian building loomed ahead, a sleek three-story edifice of glass and chrome in Palo Alto.

Silicon Valley, a place she'd only heard about in tech circles, was now her battleground. It was a far cry from the dusty streets of Baghdad where she had once navigated through market crowds, tailing insurgents without them ever noticing. Here, the enemy wore tailored suits instead of combat gear, and the weapons were lines of code rather than AK-47s.   Rose walked up to the building, holding onto her stylish leather briefcase. She planned to stride into the Lydian building looking every bit the sexy businesswoman, someone who fit right in at the sleek office block and wouldn't draw any suspicion.

Opportunity struck when Rose saw a frazzled woman struggling with files, coffee, a purse, and a suitcase. The woman dropped a file, and Rose quickly stepped in. "Let me help you with that," she said, bending down.

"Oh, thank you," the woman replied, her cheeks flushed. "I'm having such a rough day." The suitcase tipped over. "See what I mean?"

"Don't worry, I totally get it," Rose said sympathetically.

As the woman straightened up, Rose handed her the file, stealthily unclipping the laminated ID card from her waist. The woman, oblivious, thanked her and turned to grab her coffee.

Rose walked up the paved path toward the entrance, surrounded by blooming trees and landscaped gardens. She moved quickly, aware the woman might soon notice her missing ID.

A uniformed security guard stood on the other side of the revolving door. Rose sized him up: six-foot-two, muscular but a bit flabby. Threat level: moderate.

She slid the stolen ID through the scanner and flashed a bright smile at the guard, diverting his attention from the monitor. The machine beeped.

"Good morning, Reggie," she called, having noted his name badge earlier.

"Morning, ma'am," he replied, grinning as she passed. The man behind her scanned his card, the machine beeping again.

Rose entered the gleaming foyer with its high ceilings, marble floors, and metallic phoenix statue. Sunlight streamed through the tinted glass ceilings, creating an underwater effect.

Scanning the lobby for exits, she saw only the entrance behind her. The reception desk to her left was busy with people getting visitor cards. A directory was written in gold above the desk. She quickly found Damian Clayton's office on the third floor and headed to the elevator.

Inside the elevator, she observed her fellow passengers—most wearing glasses, likely from long hours at their computers. She couldn't understand the appeal of staring at code all day. To her, it felt like spending hours in a glorified prison cell.

The elevator doors swished open and she stepped out into a plush, air-conditioned corridor. Rose scanned the doors for Clayton's office, noting the lack of visible CCTV cameras. Not that it mattered; she'd be in and out before anyone realized the threat.

The CEO's office, as expected, was at the end of the corridor. She pushed open the glass door, conducting a quick risk assessment. A blonde receptionist in a chic trouser suit, her hair up in a tight bun, stood at the printer. Two burly security guards flanked the CEO's door. Ex-military, two-hundred pounds, packing.

Threat level: high.

The guards checked her out, then relaxed, assuming she wasn't a threat.

Big mistake.

"Can I help you?" the receptionist asked.

"I'm here to see Mr. Clayton." Rose flashed the stolen ID. "Sarah Flannagan from Finance."

"You don't have an appointment."

"No, but Damian asked me to bring some figures up." She rolled her eyes. "You know how he is—wants everything yesterday."

The receptionist gestured to the sofa. "I'll let him know you're here."

"Thank you."

Rose sat down, observing the guards. They wore earpieces and stared straight ahead. She tapped out a message on her phone to Anna, the admin assistant at Blackthorn Security HQ in Washington D.C. Moments later, the phone behind the desk rang.

"Hello. Mr. Clayton's office," the receptionist answered.

"What?" An urgency to her voice. "Okay, I'll send them down."

She hung up and addressed the guards. "There's been a report that someone was seen tampering with Damian's car. There's a ticking sound coming from underneath. It could be a bomb."

The guards dashed out.

Fools.

The receptionist appeared frazzled.

"Something wrong?" Rose asked, from the couch.

"No. I mean yes, but I'm sure it's okay."

Rose nodded. "All this extra security can't be easy."

"It's not. I'm totally frazzled."

"I can imagine," Rose said sympathetically. "If you want a tea break, I'll be fine here."

"Oh, I'm okay, thanks. But I think I'll use the restroom."

Rose gave a friendly nod.

The receptionist left. Rose waited half a minute then followed, taking an item out of her purse. Bending down, she slid a wedge under the restroom door. Satisfied it couldn't be opened from the inside, she returned to Clayton's office.

Opening her briefcase, she took out her Glock, savoring the cold steel in her hand. Tiptoeing to Clayton's office door, she listened.

Silence.

He was alone.

Slowly, she turned the handle and stepped inside.

"Who are you?" Clayton asked, looking up from his desk. "Where's Christine?"

Rose entered, the pistol hanging at her side.

Clayton saw it and leaped out of his chair. He was fit, not the geek she expected.

Six two. A hundred and fifty pounds. Threat level: moderate.

"Who are you?" the CEO demanded, eyeing the gun.

No fear, just anger.

Surprising.

She raised the weapon. "I'm the woman who's going to kill you."

ABOUT THE AUTHOR

Gemma Ford is a romantic suspense novelist who enjoys writing about feisty, independent women and their brave, warm-hearted men. *Duty Bound* is the first book in Gemma's Blackthorn Security romantic suspense series.

You can browse the rest of the series or sign up to Gemma's mailing list for discounts, promos and the occasional freebie at her website: www.authorgemmaford.com.